Other books by Katherine Hetzel

StarMark
Kingstone

The Chronicles of Issraya

Book 1: Tilda of Merjan

Tilda
and the
Mines of Pergatt

Katherine Hetzel

Tilda
and the
Mines of Pergatt

THE CHRONICLES OF ISSRAYA, BOOK 2

Dragonfeather Books
Bedazzled Ink Publishing Company • Fairfield, California

978-1-949290-44-8 paperback

Cover Design
by

DESIGNS

Dragonfeather Books
a division of
Bedazzled Ink Publishing, LLC
Fairfield, California
http://www.bedazzledink.com

In memory of P J G Hetzel, and all those lost to Covid 19.

Chapter 1

Lessons

BY TILDA'S TWENTY-SIXTH attempt to produce an illuminorb, Silviu's patience was wearing thin.

"Concentrate, Tilda," the Ambakian powermage snapped.

"I *am* concentrating." Tilda rubbed her palm against her trouser leg. It felt hot; surely she must've been close to pulling the Power down that time.

"Again." Silviu grabbed Tilda's hand and pulled her arm straight out in front of her.

Tilda gritted her teeth. She'd never get the hang of this. She could feel the Power inside, fizzing through her veins as it had done ever since her initiation, but she couldn't seem to pull it outside of herself to form one of the illuminated spheres that Silviu had demonstrated so easily.

Silviu sighed and rubbed his forehead. "Remember what I told you. Say the words illuminarka spherus, imagine a channel in your arm and direct the Power along it, towards your hand. Then you can shape the Power into something more tangible—like an orb."

"And if I can't?"

Silviu's blue eyes shone like chips of ice. "You must. You cannot progress any further with your training as a powermage until you succeed."

And how long would he be prepared to wait for that? Tilda's stomach dropped into her boots. If she failed to achieve this first step in her training, would Silviu start looking for another mage to represent Merjan?

She wouldn't be beaten by a little ball of light. She squared her shoulders, closed her eyes, and focussed on the fizzing sensation. It had been strange to feel that extra something inside her body over the last few days, and its constant presence had fooled her into thinking it would be easy to use the Power. But to consciously tune into that sensation and draw on it to produce an orb was much harder than it looked.

That's when the doubt demons struck; you can't do it, they screamed in Tilda's head.

Don't think about failing, a little voice replied. You can see and sense the Power—heck, you've even spoken to it. You can't give up, not after everything you've gone through to become the Mage of Merjan. Concentrate . . . and try again.

Tilda took a deep breath and quieted her thoughts. She imagined a line, running from her chest to her shoulder, then along her arm, thickening where it reached her palm. Concentrating hard, she visualised the fizzing as blue light, and gently, drew it along the line, colouring her whole arm blue. When the light also filled her palm, she imagined shaping and moulding it into a sphere.

"Illuminarka spherus," she muttered, and opened one eye to see what, if anything, had happened.

Floating just above her palm was a pea-sized ball of brilliant white light.

"I've done it!" Tilda experienced a split second rush of elation. Then the miniature orb exploded with a bang, showering her shirt sleeve in blue sparks. "Oh!"

"Extellerinq," Silviu snapped, and the sparks flashed and disappeared. "That," he frowned, "is why you need to concentrate. As soon as you stop focussing, the Power is able to escape your will and lose form, shattering into sparks which will mark whatever they come into contact with. Like your shirt."

Tilda's cheeks burned as she inspected the damage; a dozen or more tiny holes smouldered on her sleeve. "I did it though, didn't I?"

"You did. You managed to create a very small illuminorb. Now you need to be able to maintain the shape of it and increase its size." Silviu grabbed his jacket from the back of the chair and pulled it on. Then he picked up a large book from his desk. "Just remember, Concentration, focus—"

"—and feeling." Tilda scowled at the scorchmarks. Aunt Tresa wouldn't be pleased when she saw them. "Are we done for today?"

"I think so. We'll stop by the Ring Room on the way out, top you up."

Top her up? He made her sound like a jug.

"You'll be using up more Power at first as you practise. You will need to make contact with your portion more frequently in these first few months," Silviu explained.

Tilda's eyes widened. "You mean I can go and get more Power any time I want to?"

"No, I do not mean that," Silviu replied sharply. "I mean that, as I deem it necessary, I will supervise your connection and allow you to draw Power for a short time only." He peered into her face. "At least until I am confident that you know what to do. Safely, and on your own. Is that clear?"

She nodded. "Clear."

"Good. Let's get you topped up, then."

It was darker in the Ring Room than the last time Tilda had been in it, mainly because a huge tarpaulin had been stretched across the gaping space where the glass ceiling used to be. And yet, with little more than a snap of his fingers, Silviu produced six illuminorbs which flooded the room with light.

"Show-off," Tilda muttered under her breath.

"Did you say something?" Silviu was already halfway to the Ringstone.

"Never said a word."

Above the Ringstone hung a faint silvery haze, an indicator of the Power running through the conduit of five linked silviron rings.

Tilda stepped onto the pentagon of golden tiles at the base of the Ringstone. How different would this drawing of Power be to when she was initiated? "What do I do?"

"Same as before. Touch the ring and your portion of Power will be released."

"Don't I have to say anything?"

Silviu tucked the book more securely under his arm. "Not on these occasions. You will find the Power responds easily to your touch and can be drawn without incantations. I shall monitor the situation. You will feel me indicate when you should disconnect."

Tilda reached her hand out and touched the cold silver-grey metal. At once, a blue flame appeared above the Ringstone and the Merjanian Power surged through her body and left her breathless. Would she ever get used to this?

Back so soon, Tilda Benjasson, Mage of Merjan? The Power's voice in Tilda's head was more like the sound of gentle waves lapping at a pebbled shore than the roaring storm waves of her first encounter with it. The blue flame wrapped itself around Tilda's fingers, almost like a handshake.

"Yes. I'm topping up. I've been practising illuminorbs," she replied silently.

Ah, your first lessons. Have you been successful?

Tilda pulled a face. "Sort of. I only made one. It was very small. And it didn't last long either." She felt a vibration in her chest. Was the Power laughing at her?

It never does, to begin with. Do not worry, my little mage. I will be here when you need me. Let me fill you . . .

The flame grew until it enveloped Tilda in a blue aura; she closed her eyes and concentrated on the Power as it ran through her hand, up her arm, and into her chest. Every nerve tingled, she was stronger, able to produce a million illuminorbs if she had to—

A hand landed on her shoulder, forcing her to open her eyes. Silviu was mouthing "enough" at her.

"I have to go," Tilda told the Power.

Until next time, Tilda. The blue light shrank and drew back towards the Ringstone.

The light winked out, leaving Tilda with an unexpected sense of loss. Slowly, she took her hand away from the obelisk.

"That should keep you going for a few more lessons," Silviu said. "Come, it's almost time to eat. You must be hungry, I know I am."

He gestured towards the door, and with one last look at the Ringstone—devoid now of any coloured light and with only the silvery haze floating above it again—Tilda followed.

"How often do you normally need to refill?" she asked.

"Not very often, usually. But in light of what happened recently, the rest of us are also using up Power more quickly than we anticipated. We are planning to refill tomorrow, probably after your next practise. You saw for yourself how dangerous it can be to take on too much at once—"

Tilda shivered and the ghost of the smell of burning flesh filled her nostrils again. How could she *ever* forget how dangerous it was, after seeing Luisa's hands branded? Luisa had tried to take all five portions of Power for herself in revenge for not being chosen as Mage of Ambak, but hadn't reckoned on the Power fighting back. When she failed and magicked herself away from the scene, four mages had fought hard to contain the Power after it exploded out of the Ringstone. If Tilda hadn't stepped forward and joined them, they might all have been killed . . .

"—so we are pacing ourselves," Silviu continued. "We've allowed the first lot of Power, drawn during your initiation, to heal our hurts. The next filling will help us to reach normal levels."

They reached the door, where Silviu gave a twist of his fingers. The illuminorbs faded, leaving the Ring Room in gloom once more.

Tilda found herself being ushered into the corridor.

"This afternoon, I have some other matters to attend to." Silviu closed the door to the Ring Room behind him. "I suggest that you make a start on reading this." He thrust the book he'd brought with him towards Tilda.

It was unexpectedly heavy and she almost dropped it. "The Power and its Legends," she read from the cover.

"Yes. You are already aware of some of the legends associated with the Power in Ambak after your unplanned visit to that region." He ignored Tilda's sigh. "It would be good to widen your knowledge of legends from the other regions of Issraya too, but refresh yourself as to those relating to Ambak first. We'll discuss them tomorrow morning. Nine o'clock."

Tilda's arms were already aching from the weight of the book. "Can we practise illuminorbs again, too?"

"Definitely."

She hugged the book to her chest. Maybe tomorrow, she'd get it right.

Chapter 2
Practise Makes Perfect

TILDA ARRIVED IN the rooms that were her home on Ring Isle as Aunt Tresa was carrying a steaming pot to the table.

"Just in time. Wash your hands if you need to and sit yourself down." Tresa set the pot on a waiting trivet. "Hungry?"

"Starving." Tilda dropped the book Silviu had given her onto a couch and hurried over to the table, mouth watering as the smell of chicken stew hit her nose. Thank Power. She liked fish—didn't have much choice, living on an island in the Inner Sea—but it made a pleasant change to have meat from the mainland every now and again.

"You seem to be keeping Silviu busy." Uncle Vanya picked up the bread knife and cut thick slices from a crusty loaf. "I've not seen him all morning. How are the lessons going?"

Tilda took a slice of bread from the plate and bit into it. "Slowly," she said with her mouth full.

Vanya nodded. "These things take time. Remember, most mages are aware of the Power and begin to get a feel for how it works long before they are initiated as adults. You've not had that advantage."

"I managed an illuminorb, at last. About this big." Tilda pinched her fingers together to show him.

"Well done." Tresa ladled some stew into a bowl and held it out. "I should think that—"

Tilda reached out to take it.

Tresa's eyes widened. "What on earth happened to your shirt?"

"Oh." Tilda should've known Tresa would spot the burns. "The orb . . . sort of . . . exploded."

"What!" The ladle landed in the stew with a splash. Tresa put her hands on her hips and rounded on her husband. "Vanya, you didn't tell me the lessons could be dangerous. What will we tell your sister if Tilda goes up in flames? And why isn't Silviu protecting Tilda more? You'll have to talk to him and—"

"Tresa, calm." Vanya gestured to his wife to pick up the ladle again. "Silviu knows what he's doing. I'm sure Tilda is perfectly safe."

"Safe? When her sleeve's all burnt up?"

Tilda winced as Tresa slopped stew into a second bowl. "It's only a few little holes. Nothing major. I'll get better the more I practise. In fact, I might try again later, see if I can hold the form for longer."

"There'll be no trying, not here." Vanya wagged the bread knife at her. "You need to have a mage present, in case anything goes wrong." He leaned closer. "And I don't think your aunt's nerves would stand it," he whispered loudly, with a wink.

"You're not wrong there," Tresa snapped, banging her own bowl down on the table. "I'll patch that sleeve for you later, Tilda." She sniffed loudly. "Now, shall we say thanks?"

When the final drop of meaty gravy had been wiped up with the last of the bread, the table cleared and the bowls washed and put away, Tilda found herself at a loose end. Uncle Vanya had gone to see if Silviu needed anything now that he'd finished Tilda's lessons for the day, and Aunt Tresa had shut herself into her workroom with the scorched shirt.

The afternoon stretched out in front of Tilda, long and lonely. But then her eyes fell on the book of legends and she picked it up with a sigh. It was old and heavy, and she could think of a hundred things she'd rather do instead, but she ought to get some reading done. Silviu wasn't going to forget to ask her about the Ambakian legends, was he?

In her bedroom, Tilda threw herself onto her bed and lay on her stomach, the book propped open on the pillow. She ran a finger down the index.

The Finding of the Ambakian Ring. The Nargan's Lair. Mage Margoletta the First. The Black Ruby. The Hanging Rock of Kradlock. The Oxala and the Bear. There were more legends listed, but she'd begin with the Ambakian ones. She turned to The Finding of the Ambakian Ring and started reading, though she didn't really need to; she'd relived this legend so very recently.

It had started when Yaduvir tried to draw all the Power to himself at his initiation, which Silviu had prevented by using the Power to send the Ambakian ring away, back to its home region, in an attempt to protect the Ringstone. With Ring Isle isolated by powerful dark magic, it was Tilda who had mistakenly been transported to Silviu's berry farm through his Power-enchanted journal instead of the mage himself. There, in the mountains of Ambak miles away from Ring Isle, Tilda had met Neesha, Silviu's daughter, and the giant bodyguard, Abchar. With their help, and thanks in part to this very legend, Tilda had found the ring at the source of the Ambak River and returned it to Ring Isle, where she was plunged into another battle over the Power. And because of *that*, she'd ended up becoming the youngest powermage in the history of Issraya.

Tilda flipped over and stared at the ceiling. She'd bet her boots that Neesha wasn't stuck inside reading a book. Silviu's daughter would be in the mountains she loved, hunting or fishing or hiking with Abchar beside her.

It wasn't fair. Tilda itched to be doing something, too. There was all this Power inside her, fizzing away; it was hardly worth being called a powermage if all she was allowed to do was read. She should be doing something with it, like practising making illuminorbs.

She sat up suddenly. Vanya might have said she shouldn't practise, but Silviu hadn't, had he? And Silviu was her guide at the moment in all things mage-related. He hadn't told her not to practise . . .

She could try creating another orb. Yes, there was a chance it might explode, but it hadn't done too much damage before, had it?

It was the work of a few moments to roll up the rug and push both that and the wooden storage chest against the wall, leaving a wide empty space—free of anything that might catch fire or be damaged by sparks—in the middle of Tilda's bedroom floor. If she rolled her sleeves up, there wouldn't even be any incriminating scorch marks . . .

With everything ready, all she needed now were the right words. What were they again?

"Illuminarka spherus and . . . extellerinq," Tilda murmured, hoping she wouldn't need the second one much. Her heart fluttered in her chest. Should she really do this?

Yes, if it meant she could speed up her training.

For the twenty-eighth time today, Tilda spoke the words and imagined the line along her arm. She kept her eyes open this time. Maybe, if she could see what was happening in her hand, she'd be able to control the orb better. She drew the fizzing Power down the line, and—

Was that a slight shimmer in the air above her outstretched palm? It was!

Tilda wrapped her concentration around the shimmer, moulding and shaping it until suddenly, she held a pea-sized light in her palm again.

"Extellerinq," she whispered before it could explode, and the orb winked out.

Silently, Tilda danced around the room in celebration. She'd done it! Held an illuminorb without it losing its form. Breathless, she stopped. Could she do it again, make it bigger? Last longer?

It turned out she could. As the afternoon wore on, Tilda tried over and over again, until the ball of light in her palm was almost the size of her fist. She could even maintain the shape for a minute or so at a time. Tilda stared at the latest orb she'd created almost without thinking. What would Silviu say tomorrow when she showed him? He'd be really pleased and she'd be able to—

"Tilda!"

The orb exploded. Blue sparks landed on the bedspread, setting several places alight.

"Extellerinq," Tilda gasped, leaping off the bed. She flung her window open and wafted at the smoke.

Just in time; the door opened.

"Tilda, do you want to—" Tresa's eyes narrowed and she sniffed. "Why can I smell burning?"

"Um . . ." Tilda couldn't help glancing towards her bed.

"You set fire to your bed?" Tresa marched over and snatched up the burnt material. "Look at the state of this!"

"I'm sorry, but I wanted to practise and—"

Tresa's lips were a thin line. "You might be a powermage, Tilda, but you can't simply use the Power whenever you feel like it. What would you have done if this"—she held up the bundle of fabric—"had gone up in flames?"

"Thrown it out the window into the sea?" Tilda murmured, but her aunt wasn't listening.

"Wasting Power like that," Tresa muttered, heading for the door. "It's not right."

"It's not a waste if I'm learning. Anyway, I'll just top my Power up again, like I did this morning."

Tresa spun round, her eyes blazing. "Oh, you will, will you? And how will you explain that to Silviu? Even I know that the mages don't refill unless they've had a jolly good reason to use their Power. I don't reckon he'll think practising making pretty lights—alone and unsupervised—a good reason, do you? It'd serve you right if he refused to let you fill up until you learnt to follow the rules." And with that, she swept out of the room, taking the bedspread with her.

Tilda sank onto her bedspread-less bed. Oh, Power. Aunt Tresa was right—Silviu was going to be so angry, wasn't he? Especially if she'd used up all the Power she had, only a few hours after her last drawing. With a sickening jolt, Tilda realized the energetic fizzing she'd almost grown used to was now barely more than a tingle. If she was unable to produce anything at all tomorrow, she'd have some serious explaining to do. The thought of having to ask Silviu if she could draw Power to top up her residual levels sent a shiver down her spine.

She'd have to come clean, admit what she'd done.

Unless . . .

She could always top up on her own, without Silviu knowing.

Tilda chewed her lip. Could she? *Should* she? She'd seen firsthand what happened when one person tried to take control of all the Power. But that wasn't what she was trying to do, was it? She wouldn't be trying to take control—she only wanted to connect with her own portion, and she knew how to do that.

Would she be able to get into the Ring Room though? She couldn't remember Silviu locking the door when they left, only closing it, but if he had . . . Well, she'd have no option but to own up to her secret illuminorb-creating. If he hadn't . . . She'd be able to sneak in, and no one would be any the wiser.

She still needed a reason to go out though. One that Aunt Tresa would believe.

Tilda's eyes fell on the book of legends lying on her pillow. Would a trip to the library work? Better find out. She scooped up the book and hurried to her aunt's workroom.

The bedspread was already laid out on the work table and Tresa was shaking her head over it.

Standing in the doorway, Tilda felt a stab of guilt. Perhaps the damage was worse than she'd realised. "Um, Aunt Tresa? I'm sorry about the burns. I promise I won't practise any more."

Well, not where anyone will see me, or where I might set things on fire, she added silently.

Tresa looked up. "See that you don't. I want these to be the last burns I patch up."

"Silviu set me some reading." Tilda held the book up as proof. "I'm going to the library for a bit."

Tresa's attention had already moved back to the bedspread; she was sizing up scraps of fabric against the holes. "Don't be late."

"I'll be back in time for supper."

Thank Power it had been so easy. Trying not to run, Tilda slipped out of the apartment.

Chapter 3

A Nasty Surprise

HER HEART WAS pounding by the time she reached the Ring Room. She'd made a detour of course; she could now say in all honesty to anyone who asked that she really *had* been to the library. She'd even taken out another book—*A Brief History of the Island of Issraya*, which looked anything but brief—to add credibility.

Tilda held her breath and grasped the door handle. Slowly, she twisted it. Thank Power; it wasn't locked. Her luck was in. She glanced up and down the corridor to make sure there was no one around, then slipped inside.

She hadn't realised how dark the Ring Room would be without any orbs illuminating it, especially underneath the balcony. She hesitated. Had anyone else found the door unlocked? Might they be lurking in the darkness? A shiver ran down her spine as she remembered she didn't have enough Power for an orb to push the shadows back. She'd make certain from now on that she never drained so completely again, that she always had something in reserve.

The only light available came from the silvery haze above the Ringstone, and before her courage failed her, Tilda ran quickly towards it, set the books down on the golden tiles, and stared down at the five interlinked silviron circles.

She was proud to see that "her" ring—the Merjanian one closest to the blue mosaic triangle set into the floor—looked brighter than the other four as she reached for it. As soon as contact was made, the blue light enveloped her hand and the Power spoke.

Back again, Tilda? That was quick.

The voice inside her head sounded amused; Tilda thought her reply. "Yes. Sorry. I was practising illuminorbs and I think I've used up everything I took earlier. I need to draw more, until I'm back to the same level . . ."

Without another mage present? The voice was stern.

Tilda squirmed. "Just this once. I'll be careful. Please?" She waited, but the Power did not answer. Was it going to refuse?

Very well.

The blue light flared and the Merjanian portion of Power poured into Tilda, running smoothly up the imagined channel in Tilda's arm instead of down, the fizzing energy branching out and filling her.

Except something wasn't right. The intensity of the blueness in the aura was fading, and there was a heaviness in the Power's movement.

A question flashed into Tilda's mind. "Power . . . what's happening? What's wrong?"

Luisa . . .

"Where?" Tilda whipped her head round, looking for the enemy.

Her portion's voice grew softer, fainter. *She tainted our conduit . . .*

Tilda's chest tightened until she could barely breathe. "What do you mean?"

We cannot flow . . . as well as we should. Mend the conduit.

Abruptly, the Power fell silent and what remained of the blue aura disappeared back into the Ringstone.

Tilda jerked her hand away. Mend the conduit? How? What had Luisa even done to break it? All the rings were here, linked together as they were supposed to be. And the Power was still flowing through it. She stretched her hand back over the ring, determined to ask. Then she hesitated. What if the next time she made a connection, she made things worse and the Power stopped flowing altogether? How could she ever explain that to Silviu? She would go down in history as the mage who stopped the Power from working, and she'd seen what happened to mages when they were drained of Power.

She stared down at the rings. Hers was still the brightest by far—the others looked as though they were in shadow. And then she saw them; patches of darker grey in the normal colour of the duller rings. Areas that could be easily mistaken for shadow—except that shadows didn't usually affect the silver sparkles which were an integral part of the silviron. And shadows didn't usually have specks of purple-blackness in their centres. She looked closer; there was a small shadow on *her* ring, and as she watched, the purple-black speck in it swelled in size until it was the size of a grain of rice.

She gasped and fell back from the Ringstone.

That colour! The memory of it was as vivid now as it had been the first time she'd seen it, when Luisa's skin had crawled with light, but her body had been surrounded by a bruised-looking aura of purple-black.

And that dark aura had been drawn down into the Ringstone as the Power fought back against Luisa . . .

The door to the Ring Room rattled. Someone was coming!

Tilda snatched up the books and ran into the shadows under the balcony as the door opened. As an illuminorb burst into life, she leapt behind the nearest pillar and pressed her back against it, hugging the books close to her chest.

"It seems I spend far more time in here than anywhere else at the moment, Maddi."

That was Kamen, Kradlock's mage. Was he here to top up, too? Slowly, carefully, Tilda peered around the pillar.

"You need to heal," Kamen's steward replied. "Once you are full well—"

"I know, I know. Let's get on with it, shall we?"

Both Kamen and Maddi had their backs towards Tilda, but her heart was beating so loud she was sure they'd hear it and turn round.

A golden glow rose from the Ringstone, indicating that Kamen had made contact with his portion and was drawing Power.

Tilda ducked back behind the pillar, and breathed more easily. Thank Power Kamen hadn't noticed the unlocked door, or seen her dashing across the room. She'd wait for him to finish and sneak out when he'd gone. Except . . . She went cold. If she waited until he'd finished and he locked the door on the way out, she'd be trapped in the Ring Room. And being discovered here, in defiance of Silviu's orders, was somehow a worse prospect at this moment than going to Silviu voluntarily and owning up to what she'd done.

He was going to be angry, of course he was, but she couldn't keep what the Power had told her to herself. Perhaps Silviu's anger would quickly be redirected towards Luisa for tainting the conduit, rather than focusing on Tilda for disobeying him?

Tilda held her breath and tiptoed silently into the deepest shadows under the balcony. When she was certain neither Kamen or Maddi had seen or heard anything, she kept close to the wall and circled her way round to the door.

In the safety of the corridor, she leaned against the wall, her knees weak with relief. She'd managed that part of her plan—now she had to find Silviu. She took a deep breath, pushed away from the wall, and hurried in the direction of his rooms.

She met Uncle Vanya before she was even half way there.

He eyed her suspiciously. "Tilda? Where've you been?"

She held up the books. "Library, but I have to see Silviu. I need to tell him—"

"Silviu's asked not to be disturbed for the rest of the day. He's finalising plans for the expansion of his berry farm."

"But it's important, about—"

"No interruptions," Vanya stated bluntly. "At all. You will not disturb the mage. And that's an end to it."

Tilda bit back her angry response. Her uncle seemed to have forgotten that she was a mage, too. She was sure Silviu would understand why she needed to see him, and for a moment she fully intended to go to him, regardless of what Vanya said.

Her heart sank as she realised that no, Silviu probably wouldn't understand, and would send her from his apartment with a flea in her ear before she even had a chance to tell him about the affected Ringstone.

"Almost supper time," she heard Vanya say. "Let's see what your aunt's got for us, shall we? Might be a make-do meal if she's been mending your shirt this afternoon."

All the way back to their apartment, Tilda told herself she'd tried. She had. She only had to wait until tomorrow. That's when she'd tell Silviu. Nothing awful was going to happen overnight, was it? Everything would be fine . . .

Chapter 4
Confession

"AND I AM pleased to report that Tilda has created her first illuminorb, even if it didn't last very long."

Tilda tried to smile as the other powermages applauded her.

"Well done." Duska smiled. "It will get easier, in time."

Taimane nodded. "Took me a week to make my first one, and I burnt this off in the trying." He twirled the ends of his waxed moustache. "Mind, that was a few years ago now."

There had been no time for practising orbs this morning. Tilda had received a message to say that Silviu had called a meeting of the mages in the Talking Chamber. Lessons would have to wait until later, but that wasn't what was worrying her; she was more concerned about what she still had to tell Silviu—and when to do it.

The Talking Chamber was richly decorated with coloured tapestries in geometric designs, had a view of the Ring Room tower which would be all the better when the crystal dome was repaired, and a ceiling painted with a map of Issraya. A circular table dominated the chamber, its top painted to mimic the mosaic floor of the Ring Room. There were some subtle differences in the design, though; the rays of the five pointed star were painted in the colours of the Issrayan regions and outlined in gold like on the floor, but the central pentagon—formed where the rays touched and in which the Ringstone stood—was black rather than gold, and the five interlocked rings within the pentagon were silver paint, not silviron.

Each coloured ray of the star pointed towards a chair, and in each chair sat a mage. Tilda, sitting at the sharp end of the blue ray, glanced round the table.

The green ray pointed at Duska, Mage of Pergatt. Today, her red hair was pulled back from her face, held captive in a net studded with glittering green stones whose colour matched the fabric of her shirt. The purple ray pointed at Taimane, and at the Narganian dragon's head peeping over the table edge where the mage had leaned his walking stick. Kamen's coat of mustard yellow—the colour associated with Kradlock—almost outshone the yellow ray pointing in his direction. Poor Kamen. New lines had appeared on his face since his encounter with Luisa, and his dark skin could not hide the darker shadows under his eyes.

"The next issue will be for Tilda to decide who she would like to ask to be her steward," Silviu continued from his place at the end of the star's red ray. "Neesha fulfilled the role admirably at the initiation ceremony, but as she has returned to Ambak, and neither she or Tilda seemed to want that as a permanent arrangement . . ."

Was he disappointed? Tilda stared down at the painted table top. Silviu might have preferred her to choose his daughter, but Tilda knew in her heart that it wouldn't have worked. They were too different, her and Neesha, and she couldn't imagine Neesha wanting to give up her adventurous life to become little more than a servant—albeit the servant of a powermage. No, she'd have to find someone else. Problem was, who?

"There's no need to rush the child." Kamen looked at Tilda. "My Maddi took a while to find, but I wouldn't be without her. She keeps me grounded, is part best friend, part servant, part advisor. You'll know when you've found the right person for you, Tilda. They'll be the person you need them to be, whether that's bodyguard, friend, dresser, advisor, travel companion, messenger, ceremonial supporter . . . The list of their qualities goes on."

"The Power will help you to decide." Silviu steepled his fingers. "At the moment, I think it is acceptable that you are looked after by a combination of your family and ourselves, but rest assured we will all be looking out for possible candidates. And you must tell us if you think you've found someone suitable."

Tilda nodded. "I will."

Silviu looked around the table. "So, if there is no other business to discuss . . . ?"

Only the fact that Luisa had contaminated the silviron rings and the Power was struggling to flow.

But of course Tilda couldn't just blurt that out, could she?

She fidgeted in her seat, trying to decide how best to broach the subject, and whether it was better to tell all the mages at the same time or wait until Silviu was on his own.

Kamen cleared his throat. "I do have one other thing, if I may?"

"Of course." Silviu gestured to him to continue.

Kamen's caterpillar brows drew together in a frown. "I think there's something wrong with the Ringstone."

More than one mage sucked in a sharp breath, which masked Tilda's own gasp. Kamen already knew? Had he felt the same change in the Power that she had? Or had his portion had told him directly, like hers? She held her breath, waiting for him to say more.

Taimane leaned forward. "What makes you say that?"

"Like all of us, I have had reason to draw from my portion rather more frequently of late." Kamen shrugged apologetically. "What can I say? It seems that these old bones of mine do not like forcing raw Power back to its source. As a result, my healing following that event has been rather slower than I could have anticipated. Being drained so completely makes it much more difficult." He sighed. "Which also makes me realise that you will soon have to think of who my successor will be—" He held up a hand when Duska started to protest. "I am merely stating facts, my dear."

"Let's leave your age out of this for the moment," Taimane snapped. "The Ringstone's rather more important."

Silviu leant forward too, his body tense. "Please, Kamen. Tell us why you think something's wrong."

Kamen pulled himself more upright in his chair. "All was well at Tilda's initiation, and we filled to capacity then, did we not?"

The other mages nodded.

"But as I have said, my Power drained more rapidly than I expected afterwards, and I have found it necessary to draw a little every day. Most recently, my portion has seemed harder to draw, and there is discolouration of the silviron in my ring. A darkness of some kind."

"Darkness? In the metal?" Silviu frowned.

Taimane tugged at his moustache. "What could cause that?"

"Luisa," Tilda said without thinking.

"I'm sorry, Tilda. What did you say?"

Silviu's quiet voice unnerved Tilda more than if he'd shouted at her. She swallowed hard. "Luisa could," she whispered into the silence that had fallen.

"And exactly how have you reached that conclusion?"

Maybe if she said it quickly, it wouldn't be so bad. "Um . . . myportiontoldmeyesterday."

The other mages exchanged puzzled glances, then as one, turned to stare at her.

"Yesterday?" Silviu's pale eyes were like drills, boring into her. "When you drew Power under my supervision? Why didn't you say anything at the time?"

Tilda squirmed. "Because it didn't tell me then." She looked down at her hands and began to pleat and unpleat her skirt.

"So when *did* it tell you?"

Tilda looked up and the answer stuck in her throat.

Silviu's jaw was set and his lips were a thin line. "Tilda," he said through gritted teeth. "Have you drawn Power, alone, since then?"

She gave the slightest of nods.

They looked at each other in a moment of stillness. "Do you realise how dangerous that was?" Silviu exploded out of his chair. "We never—never—allow new mages to draw alone, until we are confident that they can control themselves *and* the Power."

Tears pricked Tilda's eyes. "I had to. I'd been practising illuminorbs and I didn't want you to think I'd wasted the Power, so I—"

"You were practising? Unsupervised?" Silviu slapped a hand to his forehead. "What were you thinking?"

"I wanted to show you I could make an orb. I asked my portion for a little more Power, that's all. I—"

Silviu jabbed a finger at Tilda. "You have a lot to learn, Matilda Benjasson. Mages do not do things on their own when they are inexperienced!" His voice got louder with every word until he was shouting at her. "You do not draw Power alone until we say so. You do not practise potentially dangerous—"

"Silviu, she's only a child. You don't have to shout," Duska interrupted.

Silviu slumped heavily into his seat and covered his eyes with a hand.

"I won't do it again," Tilda said in a small voice, blinking back tears.

"No, you won't," Silviu muttered. "Because I won't give you the chance." He let out a deep breath and laid his hands—his tightly clenched fists, Tilda realised with a jolt—on the table in front of him. "Let's get back to the matter of the Ringstone, shall we? Tilda, you said your portion mentioned Luisa."

Tilda sniffed and nodded. "My portion said that she had tainted the silviron."

Taimane banged his stick on the ground and Tilda jumped. "Damn that woman!" he growled. "First she tries to steal the Power, then she affects the Ringstone."

Duska rested flat hands on the green triangle in front of her. Then she spoke quietly and carefully. "Tilda, could you have misunderstood what your portion said? Forgive me, but you are still inexperienced and—"

"No! I heard it, as clear as I'm hearing you." Tilda looked round the table at the other mages. "It said that Luisa had done something to the silviron."

"It's a possible explanation for the dark areas you saw," Taimane said to Kamen.

"Hmm. Some sort of contamination?"

"Perhaps."

"It's no good guessing." Duska looked at Silviu. "We have to find out for certain."

Silviu rubbed a hand over his chin. "An inspection of the Ringstone. Yes. If the silviron is damaged—"

"Which it is," Tilda muttered under her breath.

"—then we are all in danger." Silviu pushed his chair away and stood. "Come. We need to see for ourselves."

Chapter 5
Tainted

TILDA WAS FORCED to run a few paces every now and again to keep up with Silviu as he strode along the corridors towards the Ring Room. Servants in black and grey uniforms stepped smartly out of his way and then turned to watch in amazement the procession of mages following him through the castle.

In the Ring Room everything looked normal in the light of half a dozen illuminorbs. The usual silvery haze hung over the Ringstone, but Tilda couldn't help shivering as the mages crowded round the obelisk and leant in close.

"You're blocking the light," Kamen snapped. "Move back, for Power's sake." Grumbling, he took a glass lens from his pocket, held it to his eye, and bent low over the rings.

Tilda chewed a thumbnail. He'd be looking for those little purple-black specks in the shadows, and she had a horrible feeling that he'd find them in her ring now, too.

"There is even more silviron affected than before," Kamen said, straightening up at last. "See here, and here?" He pointed.

Taimane frowned. "What, that?" He made to touch a ring, but Silviu grabbed his hand before he could connect.

"Yes, that, Taimane. For Power's sake, don't touch it until we know what we're dealing with."

"Is it even safe to connect?" Duska's voice trembled.

Silviu looked thoughtful. "I'm not sure, although both Kamen *and* Tilda"—he shot a glare in her direction—"have drawn recently with no apparent ill effects. Let's try, but for a few moments only."

He squared his shoulders. "Tune in to your portions, take heed of anything they say, and we will compare notes afterwards." Then he looked directly at Tilda again. "Make sure you break away on my order."

She gulped and nodded.

On Silviu's signal, all five reached for their rings. Five coloured strands of light erupted from the silviron, and wrapped themselves around their respective mage's hands.

You can't . . . keep away, Tilda . . . can you? The Power's voice was faint, hesitant.

"Silviu wanted to check we can still draw, in spite of what Luisa's done."

It is getting . . . harder . . . to flow. The other . . . portions are worse.

It was true. Of the five strands, the blue appeared the strongest, its paler-than-normal light enveloping Tilda's arm to the elbow. The other four colours were barely out of the Ringstone.

I am stronger . . . but we must be equal, the Power whispered. *Or we will all . . . suffer . . . Mend the conduit—*

"Release!"

Tilda snatched her hand away, her fingers tingling. What did that mean, "I am stronger, but we must be equal?" And how could they mend the Ringstone if they didn't know exactly how it was broken?

"Well?" Silviu demanded.

"I could barely draw." Duska stared at her hand in disbelief.

"Never before have I struggled to draw my portion to me." Taimane thumped his stick on the floor. "Never!"

"Nor I," Silviu said. "Kamen?"

Kamen leaned heavily against the Ringstone. "It is as I feared. And it seems that our attempt to draw has had consequences. The shadows are growing."

It was true. As Tilda watched, one of the shadows in Silviu's ring spread further, like ink spilled on a table. She swallowed. What would the other mages think, when they asked her what her portion had felt like and she told them it had suggested that it was the strongest of the five? That she still had access to Power when the other, more experienced mages, didn't?

"My portion said it was getting harder to flow," she muttered. "And . . ." She stared at her feet and the golden tiles she was standing on; it was better than seeing the other mages' faces. "It said it was stronger than your portions, but they all had to be equal."

"Equal?" Silviu snapped.

"It said we had to mend the conduit."

Kamen frowned. "Mend it? How?"

"It's the silviron that's tainted," Silviu replied. "So—"

"We replace the silviron!" Tilda grinned. There was a solution after all.

Taimane snorted. "So all we have to do is find a lump of silviron, eh?"

Tilda looked at him and stopped grinning. "I suppose so."

"Well, that's alright then." Taimane limped around the Ringstone. "We'll nip over to Pergatt, pop down a mineshaft with a pickaxe, and dig up a lump or two."

That didn't sound too bad, but Tilda didn't like the way Taimane's moustache was bristling.

She nodded. "Yes. Then we can fix it."

"Of course we can't!" Taimane barked, rounding on her. "There was only one lump of silviron ever discovered, and it's there." He jabbed his stick towards the Ringstone. "All of it, right there. How in Power's name are we supposed to replace that silviron when there's not been a sniff of any more of the stuff in the whole of Issraya for millennia? The Ringstone will be useless!"

Everyone else started talking at once.

"The Power wouldn't tell us to mend the Ringstone if it wasn't—"

"The Historykeepers might be able to help—"

"Be calm, my old friend, and—"

Tilda stared at the other mages open mouthed. If the Power had said it could be mended, surely they ought to believe it? The mages needed to be asking questions, not quarrelling. She glanced down at the Ringstone. If they weren't going to ask, she would.

She slapped her hand down onto her ring.

Time slowed as it had before, on her very first encounter with the Power through the Ringstone. Tilda could see Silviu open mouthed, his hand moving towards her at snail's pace; Duska's eyebrows rising slowly into her fringe; Taimane's stick falling as he threw his hands into the air in slow motion.

T-T-Tilda! Have care, the Power whispered. *The taint grows.*

To the right of Tilda's hand was a shadow—a bruised ink blot—growing. She had to be quick.

"Is there more silviron?"

Yes . . .

Tilda kept one eye on the increasing contamination, hating what it was doing to her Power, but desperate to ask another question. "Where?"

There was no reply, and the nearest shadow was now only a hair's breadth from her little finger. She had no idea what would happen if it touched her skin. Panic welled up, acid hot, inside her chest. Had Luisa's contamination finally affected the Power so much that it couldn't speak to her?

The same . . . place, was a whisper so faint she almost missed it.

Someone yanked Tilda away from the Ringstone, breaking her contact. Before she could react, her arms were pinned to her sides and she was shaken so hard, her teeth rattled. She was almost deafened by shouting.

"Did you not hear me when I said how dangerous—"

"What in Power's name—"

"You little fool!"

Tilda pulled herself free of Taimane's grasp and staggered away from the Ringstone, panting. When an arm snaked around her waist she tried to push it away.

"Peace, Tilda, it's me." Duska's concerned face swam into view, and Tilda allowed herself to be supported.

"I had to find out," she gasped.

"I know, I know," Duska soothed. "But—"

"Have you seen the state of the rings after your little stunt?" Silviu yelled. "There's not a bit of silviron free of the taint. Look!"

"It doesn't matter, there's more!"

Tilda's yell finally silenced the mages, though their shouts still rang in her ears.

"Say that again." Taimane peered into her face.

"There's more silviron. My portion said so."

Kamen lurched towards her. "Where?"

"It said 'the same place,' but I didn't have time to find out where that was." Tilda clenched her fists. "I could've asked, but you didn't let me."

"There's no need. I know where the Power means." Duska's face was grim.

"This is ridiculous." Silviu paced around the Ringstone so fast, Tilda felt dizzy watching him. "There is no more silviron."

"There might be." Duska drummed her fingers on the edge of the Ringstone.

Silviu shook his head. "It's been too long. Don't you think if any more existed, it would have been discovered by now? Dug up and locked away to prevent arguments? The Power's confused by the taint, it's talking rubbish."

Tilda sucked in a breath at that. How could Silviu dismiss the Power's message so easily?

"We need to find another way to access the Power. Possibly an earthdraw."

An earthdraw? What was that? Tilda opened her mouth to ask, but the conversation moved on without her.

"We can't go back to earthdraws, surely?"

"Perhaps. We'll need to talk to the Historykeepers."

"Will the records go far enough back?"

"And even if they do, will we be able to do it?" Taimane tugged his moustache.

Tilda frowned. Do what, exactly? Why was everyone suddenly talking in riddles? She didn't understand . . .

Silviu crossed his arms. "We've a fair bit of Power still at our disposal at the moment. Kamen, will you stay here, and look for anything useful in Ring Isle's library? We three"—he pointed at himself, Taimane and Duska—"will go to Merjan City and consult the Historykeepers. Our aim will be to rediscover instructions for an earthdraw, or any other ways that Power was accessed before the Ringstone was constructed. That way we're all involved. And perhaps we'll find a way round this problem." He glanced at the Ringstone. "Agreed?"

All the mages nodded and murmured their agreement, except for Tilda. Wasn't Silviu forgetting something? She tried to catch his eye, but he was avoiding looking at her. "What about me? What shall I do?"

"You will stay here and behave yourself." Silviu's tone was icy. "I can find plenty of reading material to keep you busy until we return. And this room will be locked during our absence, just in case you had any plans in that direction."

"No!" Tilda clenched her fists and pressed them against her legs. How could they leave her out of this? "That's not fair. I'm a powermage, too. I have a responsibility to the people of Issraya. I must do something!"

"Then it's a shame you didn't think about that before you acted so irresponsibly," Taimane snapped.

Tilda's cheeks grew warm and her eyes prickled again. "But I didn't think—"

"Tilda, you're young, inexperienced." Duska spoke softly, but the words still stung. "No experienced powermage has ever had to deal with anything like this, it's all an unknown. If we can't sort it out . . . It's not just Issraya that will suffer when we can no longer protect it. There will be a physical cost to each of us as the Power we have is completely used up. Ultimately . . ."

"Initiated mages die without access to Power," Taimane finished for her.

The mages died without Power? Tilda's head reeled. Why hadn't anyone told her that? She'd almost drained herself just practising illuminorbs.

"It will be easier for us to work at finding a solution without having to worry about you," Silvia said, breaking the silence which had fallen.

She was a mage. She should be helping. "There must be *something* I can do?"

"You've not been initiated long enough to have learned to read any of the ancient writings." Kamen sounded almost apologetic.

"And illuminorbs won't be of much use." Silviu's jaw was set. "We leave tomorrow, at dawn. Inform your stewards and pack accordingly."

Through the tears sliding down her cheeks, Tilda tried again. "Can't I—"

"No." It was a simple statement of fact.

That was that, then. Tilda followed the mages to the door and wiped the wetness from her cheeks when Silviu—the last out of the Ring Room—locked the door behind him.

Chapter 6
A Stolen Fish

IT WAS STILL dark the next morning when Tilda was woken by Uncle Vanya trying to be quiet.

"For Power's sake," Tresa hissed. "You'll wake Tilda."

It was a bit too late to warn him of that. Tilda turned over and looked across the room. The window was a pale grey square in a dark wall, indicating that dawn—and the departure of the mages—must be close. It wasn't fair to be left behind. She was a powermage, too. Silviu could have let her help, even if it was just fetching and carrying for the other mages as they did their research . . .

She turned away from the window and pulled the blankets over her head, listening to the muffled noises coming from the main room. Uncle Vanya and Aunt Tresa were talking, too quietly to make out what was being said. And from the clink of plates or bowls, they must be eating breakfast.

The sounds lulled Tilda back to sleep—they must've done, because she woke from a dream where someone was knocking on her bedroom door. She yawned. What time was it?

The knocking came again, louder, more insistent. It wasn't a dream.

"Tilda? Are you awake?"

She sat bolt upright in bed. That was Kamen's voice. What in Power's name was he doing, knocking on her door?

"Hang on," she called. Wide awake now, she snatched her dressing gown from the end of her bed and pulled it on as the door opened.

Kamen stood silhouetted in the doorway. "Get dressed, quickly. You have five minutes."

"Wha—Why?"

But he'd already gone and she was talking to a closed door.

"Five minutes, Tilda," Kamen called through the wood.

She lit a candle with shaking hands, and dressed quickly. Why did she have to get up and dressed? Silviu couldn't need to see her; he'd already sent a huge pile of books to the apartment, and she hadn't had time to do anything else worth a ticking off since she left the Ring Room. She laced her boots. Perhaps Kamen was taking her down to the docks so Silviu could reinforce the fact that she was being left behind. Surely not.

But Tilda blew out the candle and took her coat from its peg anyway. Just in case.

When she walked into the main room, there was no sign of Uncle Vanya. Only Aunt Tresa, wringing her hands as she paced up and down by the table.

Tresa looked up, hurried over to Tilda, and pulled her into a hug. "Be good. Do as you're told. Try to keep out of trouble." She quickly kissed Tilda's cheek, then pushed her towards the door, where Kamen was waiting.

"Ready? Let's go." He grabbed her arm and almost pulled her down the stairs into the corridor.

"Where are we going?"

"Quiet. You'll see."

Kamen led Tilda along the familiar red and orange corridors of the Ambakian part of the castle into ones that were new to her, tiled up to waist height in blues and greys, with seascapes painted above. Was this the Merjanian quarter, where Tilda would end up living once she'd found her steward? If it was, it didn't feel very lived in. There were large padlocks on the outside of some of the doors, and for one awful moment, Tilda wondered whether Kamen had been ordered to lock her up here instead of leaving her with her aunt.

Silviu wouldn't go that far that to stop her from getting into mischief while the mages were away, would he?

It seemed not—Kamen stopped by a painting of a particularly stormy sea. "Ouvray teranta prolikiss," he said, pressing hard on a small boat which was about to be swamped by a giant wave.

The painting and tiles beneath it swung towards Tilda; she stepped back quickly. Behind the hidden door, a staircase wound down and out of sight.

"Down you go." Kamen grasped a handle on the inside of the door and waved Tilda on.

Slowly, she walked down the first few steps. The spiral staircase was lit once every turn by a small illuminorb set inside a glass lantern, the stone steps worn and uneven as though a great many people had walked this way over the years. Tilda put her hands against the rough cut walls to steady herself; they were cold and damp to the touch. Was she inside the rock on which the castle was built? Exactly how far down were they going?

There was a sharp click above her, and Tilda realised that Kamen had closed the secret door. She heard him coming down the stairs and soon his feet were at a level with her head. "Keep moving, we don't have long."

Growing dizzier with every turn, Tilda kept descending. Was it her imagination, or were the steps getting easier to see, even though the orb lamps were spaced further apart? Yes, the staircase was growing lighter and she sped up, spiralling faster and faster until there were no more steps, just an archway in the rock and the unmistakeable smell of salt and seaweed. She stepped through the arch and found herself on the dock, blinking in the brightness of the sunrise.

"Don't stop now," Kamen said. "The boat's ready to leave."

It was true. A single mooring rope, held fast by Isaak, Duska's steward, anchored the *Silver Fish*—the same boat which had brought Tilda to Ring Isle the very first time—to the tiny dock. There were no other boats, and Captain Abram raised a hand in greeting when he saw Tilda.

Duska stood beside him, dressed in a thick travelling coat.

Tilda pulled her coat tighter to ward off the chill sea breeze which was already tugging at the sails of the *Silver Fish*. "I said I was sorry," she muttered. "Did you really have to bring me down here to wave everyone off?"

"Wave everyone off? What are you talking about?" Kamen frowned at her. "You're going with Duska. Hurry, onto the boat with you."

She heard the words, but they didn't make sense. "I'm what?"

Kamen gave her a gentle push. "Duska will explain once you're under way. Quickly!"

As soon as Tilda set foot on the deck, Isaak jumped aboard with the mooring rope. The boat gave a leap and, under Abram's skilful hands, was soon heading for open water.

"Welcome, Tilda," Duska said.

There were distant shouts, and Tilda looked back at the dock. Duska moved to stand beside her.

They were far enough away not to be affected when one of the figures who'd come running onto the empty dockside shot red sparks after them.

Oh, Power. Tilda had the horrible feeling that she'd just been dragged into something. She looked up at Duska. "Have you just stolen Silviu's boat?"

"Borrowed, not stolen. And not for long. Abram's going to sail back to Ring Isle tomorrow."

Tilda glanced back, but the *Silver Fish* had rounded a rocky outcrop; the dock and castle were already out of sight. "I don't understand. Why have you left Silviu behind? And why am I here?"

"Have a seat." Duska indicated a trunk on the deck. There was a blanket lying there and she wrapped it around Tilda's shoulders before they both sat down. "That'll help keep the chill off. Warm enough?"

Tilda nodded and waited.

Duska sighed and looked out, over the waves. "You must understand that I have a lot of respect for Silviu, but in this instance, I believe he's wrong to dismiss what the Power told you. We need to explore all avenues to mend the Ringstone, and if the Power says there's more silviron with which we might make a repair, then I believe it. At the very least, we must try to find it." She looked at Tilda. "You and me, we're going to Pergatt."

Pergatt, Pa's home region. Tilda shivered and pulled the blanket tighter around her shoulders. Everything had happened so quickly this morning, she wasn't prepared for a journey to the land of forests and jewels.

"I've got nothing to take with me," she realised aloud. "How can I go all the way to Pergatt, dressed like this?"

"We will have time to purchase most of what you'll need in Merjan. The rest, we'll find in Pergatt."

"You heading back home for a while, Lady Duska?" Abram called from the steering platform. "And taking the Lady Matilda with you?"

"I am, but it's best not too many folk know of it."

Abram pulled on the steering arm. "I'm sure Lady Matilda's Ma will be glad to be told where her daughter is heading." He cleared his throat. "I'm invited for dinner this e'en."

Tilda glanced up at Abram, but he avoided her eye. Yes, she'd noticed him and Ma standing close together at her initiation. And she knew Abram had helped Ma move out of Baker Arnal's and into her new home. Of the two men, Tilda was glad it was Abram who Ma had invited to dinner.

"I'll not tell anyone else, my Lady. You have my word. On the Power."

Duska gave a brief nod. "Very well. Tell her that Tilda's travelling to her father's homeland with me. Nothing else."

Abram flashed Tilda a grin. "Aye, I'll do that." He altered the position of the steering handle. "I'm not daft. There's something serious going on. Is it to do with when we couldn't sail close to the isle?"

Tilda felt suddenly very sick. She remembered all too well the awful pressure closing in on Ring Isle as Yaduvir's dark magic isolated the island. She couldn't tell Abram about it though—everyone on Ring Isle at the time had been sworn to secrecy.

Duska stiffened beside her. "If it was, can we rely on your discretion, Captain Abram?"

"On the Power, I'll not say a word, Lady. The rest of Issraya will find out about it soon enough if things are that bad. Until then, I hope the Power keeps you safe on your travels."

Tilda hoped so, too.

Chapter 7

The Door Keepers

THE *SILVER FISH* sailed into Merjan's port late the same morning.

"It's the way it goes," Abram told Tilda as he steered the little boat towards an empty mooring point. "You can't ever tell exactly how long the journey'll take, cos the wind's her own mistress and we're at her mercy. Today, she didn't want to blow so hard."

Tilda hadn't minded. She'd eaten the biscuits Duska had brought as a make-do breakfast and actually managed to keep them down, because the lack of strong wind meant there hadn't been the swells she'd experienced on her last sailing trip. Power, how her stomach had churned that time. She wouldn't mind sailing, if every journey could be guaranteed to be as smooth as this one.

Right now, she was simply glad to be back. She hurried to the prow of the boat and stood drinking in the sight of her home city. The docks were as busy as when she'd left, with the addition of a fleet of Inner Sea boats nipping in and out of the harbour. Larger boats from far away lands were being manouevred carefully alongside the jetties. Passengers gathered in crowds, waiting patiently to board the ships being made ready for them. Merchants took stock of the cargo being run up and down gangplanks, marking their pages-long checklists. Sailors coiled ropes, swabbed decks, and rigged sails, their heads wreathed in clouds of smoke from their short-stemmed pipes.

Through all of this humanity and busyness, Isaak cleared a path for the mages. It was Tilda's first time in the city since her initiation;

Duska got nods of recognition or respectful bows as they passed through the crowds, but Tilda got pointing fingers, curious stares, and whispers. She tried to ignore it by refusing to look anywhere except at her feet.

"Walk tall, Tilda," Duska murmured. "It is what our people expect of their powermages."

Did anyone here on the docks actually think Tilda *was* a powermage? As embarassing as it was to be the centre of attention, she was willing to bet people were only taking notice of her because she was with Duska. They weren't noticing her because they thought she was a mage too. Perhaps she ought to take a lesson from Duska and start acting like one, give them something to really point at.

She pulled her shoulders back, lifted her chin, and although she couldn't bring herself—yet—to meet the curious stares, she managed to walk tall.

At the end of the dock, a carriage was waiting. Under the direction of Isaak, the trunk, which had been carried from the *Silver Fish* by a waiting dockhand, was being loaded onto its roof.

"Isaak," Duska said, "will you go ahead, say we'll be there shortly?"

"Of course. Within the hour?"

"Yes, that should be plenty of time. Can you pick up something for our lunch, too? I'm ravenous after all that sea air. Are you ready, Tilda?"

Was now the time to admit that no, she wasn't ready, because she'd never been beyond the borders of Merjan City before, let alone anywhere else in the Merjanian region? Apart from an unintended visit to the Ambakian mountains of course, but that hadn't exactly been her choice. Or to admit that, although she was an initiated powermage, she didn't feel ready because she had no idea why Duska had brought her along or what she was expecting of her, and she didn't know how to use the Power, other than to make balls of light?

And yet . . .

Duska had listened to her when Silviu hadn't. She must have decided that Tilda might be of some real use in Pergatt, even though Tilda couldn't think how. Perhaps Duska could see something in Tilda that she had yet to recognise in herself—perhaps she thought Tilda *was* ready to do some proper powermaging, even though Silviu didn't.

The only way Tilda was going to find out was if she went to Pergatt and helped to look for the silviron the Power had assured her was still there.

Tilda nodded. "Yes. I'm ready."

"Hop in, then."

Tilda scrambled inside, closely followed by Duska. Isaak shut the door, saluted, and banged three times on the side of the carriage.

The coach lurched forward; Tilda was on her way.

She stared out of the window as the driver took them deeper into the city instead of out of it. They drove down Blood Alley, where fresh sides of meat hung in the open shop windows and men in bloodied aprons sawed chops or sliced steaks. And Tin Lane, where you could buy everything from a saucepan to a bath tub and the tang of metal hung in the air. Did Duska think they had time for a tourist trip? As much as Tilda appreciated seeing the coloured fabrics fluttering in Silk Road, or gazing at the chocolate and cream confections in Pudding Row, she couldn't help thinking that they were wasting precious time. This was definitely not the fastest route to Pergatt.

The coach finally stopped in Coats Road.

"Right, let's get you some basics for the trip," Duska said, jumping down from the carriage.

Oh, of course . . . That's why they were still in the city.

The first purchase was a trunk; Tilda chose one made of greenwood with silver locks. A boy was found, who for a few coins agreed to carry the new trunk from shop to shop. After each visit, some new item of clothing was added until the boy was staggering under the weight of his load and Tilda was struggling to think of anything else she could possibly need. Duska bought leggings, trousers, a single skirt and fine blouse—"just in case"—thick woollen shirts, a pair of sturdy boots, and a pair of soft leather slippers. Socks, hat, coat, underwear, nightclothes . . . In less than an hour the trunk was full and being loaded onto the carriage. Tilda waved her thanks to the exhausted boy, and they set off again.

But still the driver did not head out of the city as she'd expected him to. Instead, he took narrower and darker roads that Tilda did not recognise.

"Um . . . shouldn't we be heading to Pergatt now? It'll take a while to get there, won't it?"

Duska nodded. "Seven days, usually."

Tilda sat up straighter. A week? "Then why are we still in the city? Aren't you worried Silviu will catch up with us before we leave?"

"He won't. We're going to see Gemsman Georj."

"Who?"

"Gemsman Georj. He's one of a handful of gemsmen operating outside of Pergatt for those unwilling or unable to make the seven day trip to the region."

"Why?"

"You'll find out when we get there."

Duska's calmness was beginning to irritate Tilda, especially when she wouldn't be drawn further on why they were visiting a gemsman before they left for Pergatt. And nothing Tilda could think of seemed to justify it either. She'd simply have to wait and see.

Isaak opened the carriage door when the coach stopped for the second time. "Georj is ready and waiting," he told Duska.

"Good. We'll go straight in."

Tilda would have followed Duska into the shop, but the gemsman's window display made her hesitate. It was only a narrow window, but set across its width were seven white pedestals of varying heights, and on top of each pedestal was a single glittering stone. Together, they formed a perfect rainbow.

Duska tapped Tilda on the shoulder. "There are more inside."

There certainly were. Tilda didn't know where to look first. White-painted, glass-fronted cabinets filled the tiny shop, and on their shelves sat hundreds of gems. Some were tiny, mere pinpricks of colour. Others were as big as a hen's egg. A few had been set into gold or silver jewellery, but most were simply stones. Stones cut, polished, and glittering with reflected light.

"Lady Duska, a pleasure, as always." Gemsman Georj took Duska's hand and kissed it.

"It's been too long, Georj. Allow me to introduce the Lady Matilda."

Tilda was relieved to see that Georj didn't seem inclined to kiss *her* hand; he bowed his head instead. The gemsman was a typically tall, slim, and auburn-haired Pergattian. He wore a dark grey pinstriped coat with three smokey grey crystals for buttons. He must have seen Tilda staring at them, because he fiddled with one.

"Ashstone," he said. "Not a very expensive gem, but unusual, and they go well with the jacket." He smiled at her, green eyes twinkling, then turned back to Duska. "Do you have time for stones, or is it straight to the strong room?"

"The strong room, please, Georj."

Georj pulled aside a curtain at the back of the shop and uncovered a doorway leading into an even smaller room, where a large lamp—unlit—hung over a curve-edged workbench. Under the bench was a set of drawers; the top drawer stood half open and Tilda peeked inside. Laid out in neat rows were tiny hammers, saws, and other tools whose shape she didn't recognise and whose use she could only guess at. Beside the bench was a rickety table piled up with navy blue boxes of varying sizes, their lids embossed with two entwined letter g's.

There was another door here, too: a metal one.

Georj took a set of jangling keys out of his pocket. He selected one, slotted it into the lock of the metal door, and turned it. There was a series of clicks, and he removed the key. Then he chose a different key and inserted it into the same keyhole. He turned this one; it made a single—loud—click, and the metal door finally swung open.

Georj smiled. "After you, Ladies."

The strong room wasn't very exciting. All it contained was a large cabinet full of narrow drawers, and a large tapestry of a woodland scene hanging on a pole across one wall. Tilda was disappointed. She'd expected to see even more glittering gems, but there were none. Perhaps they were all in the cabinet and something else was under lock and key. Maybe that's why they had to come here—to collect something valuable before they could finally set off?

"Mind your back," Isaak grunted.

Tilda stepped quickly to one side to give him room.

Isaak set Tilda's new trunk on the floor, turned, and left.

"Why is my trunk in here?"

"Because we are going to Pergatt," Duska said.

"Yes, but . . ." Tilda stared from her trunk to Duska, and back again. "The carriage is outside."

"We shan't be needing it."

Isaak came in a second time, set Duska's trunk beside Tilda's, and headed out again.

Duska reached inside her collar and pulled a long chain out from inside her shirt. "Can you draw that tapestry back for me please, Tilda?"

The tapestry was heavy, but slid back easily on its pole. Behind it was yet another door, this one with five interlocked rings burned into the pale wood above a simple handle.

Isaak came back, loaded with bags this time. These he dumped next to the trunks.

"They're the last," he said.

The strong room was feeling pretty cramped with four people and a pile of luggage in it. What in Power's name was going on?

"Open it, then," Duska said.

Tilda opened the door; behind it was a bare plastered wall. She glanced over her shoulder and saw Georj and Isaak grinning at her. Was this someone's idea of a joke?

Duska smiled. "Close it again. Now for the magic . . ." She stepped round the luggage and stood in front of the door to nowhere. Then she held up a small key attached to the chain hanging round her neck. Tilda watched closely as Duska brought the key close to the symbol burned above the handle.

"Drethtallambra Pergatt," Duska murmured.

A hole appeared—a tiny keyhole—right in the centre of the five rings.

Tilda gasped. It looked as though someone was shining a green light through the lock from the other side, yet she'd seen with her own eyes the wall behind the door . . . Was this Power being used?

Duska stepped back. "You can open it again now."

This time the door opened onto a forest. A dark and gloomy forest, filled with gnarled trunks, spring leaves, and birdsong. It smelled of damp earth and rotting vegetation; Tilda could even feel a breeze on her face.

It was real.

"Amazing what the Power can do, isn't it?" Duska laughed. "Where do you think this door takes us?"

There was only one place in Issraya it could be. "Pergatt," Tilda whispered.

"Exactly. It saves a week's travelling to go this way. Georj is not just a gemsman, you see—he's a Door Keeper."

"It's another power portal," Tilda breathed. Did each powermage have access to some secret Power-fuelled way to travel? Not so long ago, she'd travelled huge distances to Ambak through Silviu's journal . . . "How?"

"The door can only be unlocked by this key, which has Power stored in it. When the right incantation is spoken," Duska gestured at the doorway, "it opens. It's my little secret."

Isaak and Georj carried the trunks into the forest. Duska walked through too, breathed in deep, and let her breath out in a huge sigh.

"Home. I'll lock the door behind us," she told Georj as he stepped back into the strong room and passed Isaak the bags. "Power willing, we'll return the same way. Well, Tilda. Are you coming or not?"

Tilda took a deep breath. "Yes. Yes, I'm coming." And then she stepped out of the gemsman's strong room in Merjan and into Pergatt.

How odd it was, to see someone lock a door that stood all on its own in the middle of hundreds of trees.

As Duska tucked the chain and its key back inside her shirt, Tilda tried the door handle. The door opened, but showed only forest on the other side. She shut it again, and stepped back to study this strange phenomenon. It was as though someone had decided to build a house, starting with the door, before giving up and not bothering with any of the rest.

"We'll eat before we move on," Duska said. "I can hear your stomach rumbling from here, and it'll give you a chance to acclimatize to being in Pergatt."

There was a fallen tree nearby which proved to be comfortable enough; Tilda tucked into the impromptu picnic while sitting on the makeshift bench, but her eyes kept being drawn back to the door. She half-expected to see it open and for someone else to walk through. No one did though.

Eventually Duska rose and brushed the crumbs off her clothes. "Let's carry on, shall we? This way." She headed into the trees with Isaak.

Tilda hurried after them. "But what about the luggage?"

"I'll fetch it later," Isaak told her.

As they walked, Tilda saw a pattern in the dense trees, a regularity that couldn't possibly be natural. She was on a path of sorts, but where did it go?

She didn't have to wait long to find out; up ahead, the trees were thinning, the gloom growing brighter, and then she was walking into a large clearing. In the middle of it stood a log cabin, its door wide open, smoke curling up from the chimney. Someone was definitely at home.

"Hello-o," Duska called.

Two large hounds—one golden brown, one brindled red and white—bounded out of the cabin and raced towards the visitors, barking loudly. They skidded to a halt in front of Duska and bared their teeth as they growled.

Tilda would have run, but Isaak caught her arm.

"Steady," he said.

A shrill whistle sounded. The dogs fell silent and looked over their shoulders, toward the cabin. An elderly man appeared at the cabin door, two dead rabbits dangling from his hand. "Here, Oak, Flame," he called.

As one, the dogs turned and trotted back to him, their tails wagging.

Duska followed them at a slower pace. "Power bless you, Benji."

"Lady." Benji dropped the rabbits onto a table beside the door. The dogs flopped by his feet and lay grinning up at him, their tongues lolling.

"Cart's round the back?" Isaak called, letting go of Tilda's arm.

Benji nodded once and pulled a knife from his belt. "Ar."

"I'll fetch the bags, then." Isaak gave Tilda a gentle nudge in the direction of the cabin. "I assume we're stopping here the night?"

"I think so." Duska glanced towards the old man. "If that's alright with you, Benji? Digdown can wait til tomorrow."

"It is." Benji pointed at Tilda with his knife. "New maid?" With a swift movement, he lowered the knife and made an incision in one of the rabbits.

"Not exactly." Duska smiled and beckoned Tilda closer.

Tilda's back was ramrod straight as she marched over to the table where Benji was gutting the rabbit. "I am Lady Matilda, Mage of Merjan."

"That so? Huh." Benji continued his work and didn't look up. "You know how to peel tatoes?"

"Yes, but—"

"Sack of 'em inside. Get some peeled, will ya?"

Tilda's cheeks grew hot. Who did this man think he was, ordering her about? She was a mage, for Power's sake! "But I—"

"I'll show you." Duska took hold of Tilda's arm and gently steered her inside.

As Tilda's eyes adjusted, the room became clearer. This Benji must live a simple life. There was an open fireplace with various hooks and grills for cooking hanging over it; a few pans hanging from the beams, alongside game birds and bundles of onions and herbs; a single stool near a roughly hewn table, and a narrow cot bed had been pushed against a wall. In one corner was a low cupboard, surrounded by lumpy sacks, and above it were shelves stacked with preserving jars and screw-topped tins. It was definitely a home for someone who liked their own company.

"You musn't mind Benji," Duska said quietly. "I've known him for many years, and I often help him out when I stay here if I'm passing through. He doesn't mean any harm by how he speaks. It's quite refreshing, sometimes, to not have someone treat you like a powermage."

Tilda couldn't imagine that. She'd probably not been a powermage long enough to appreciate *not* being treated like one. "But who is he?"

"He's my other Door Keeper. Keeps an eye open for anyone who comes too close to this part of the forest and makes sure they don't find the actual door."

Well, that made sense, to have a Keeper on both sides of the door. Tilda glanced round the simple cabin again. "You said we were going to sleep here tonight, but there aren't enough beds."

"Not in this room, no. Isaak usually likes to sleep in the fresh air, so will bed down under the cart when he comes back. We'll be upstairs, under the eaves, where I usually sleep on my own. It should be big enough for both of us, you don't take up much room." Duska smiled and reached into one of the sacks. She pulled out a handful of potatoes, and passed them to Tilda. "Now, let's find the carrots and an onion, shall we?"

Dinner was the best tasting rabbit stew Tilda had ever eaten, and Benji's eyes crinkled at the corners when she told him so.

As they ate, Duska explained where they'd be heading the next morning. "We're going to Digdown, the biggest mining town in Pergatt. It's at the edge of this forest, about half a day's ride from here."

"Do you know where we need to start looking for"—Tilda shot a look at Benji—"you-know-what?"

Duska chuckled. "You can talk freely, Tilda. We're looking for silviron, Benji. We've been told it exists, and we need to find it as a matter of some urgency."

Benji fondled Oak's golden head. "None's been found since the first time. Could be you're lookin' for a while."

"Perhaps. I'm hoping we'll have someone to help though."

Tilda's ears pricked up at that. "Who?"

"My contacts tell me that there's a relatively new Master on the scene," Duska told her. "One Feliks Weaverson. He only has one team, but they've been digging up some of the best stones seen in ages." She looked thoughtful. "If they're that good at finding gems, maybe they'll be good enough to find silviron too."

And if they weren't? Tilda couldn't bear to think of the consequences.

Chapter 8
Digdown

THE SPACE UNDER the eaves was every bit as cosy as Duska had promised, but when Tilda first lay down that night, she couldn't relax because of the silence. Where was the sound of waves that used to lull her to sleep? And yet, as she listened, she realised the forest wasn't really silent. The rustle of leaves in the breeze sounded a little like waves on the rocks, and slowly she fell into a deep sleep, dreaming of a door in the middle of nowhere that had strange new places behind it every time she opened and closed it.

"Tilda. Tilda? Time to wake up."

She opened her eyes and yawned. There was an unfamiliar sloping roof over her head. Then she remembered and sat upright, her head missing a crooked rafter by a hairs breadth. She was in Pergatt!

"Isaak's loading the cart," Duska told her. "Get up and come down. We'll eat as we travel, to save time."

There was no sign of Benji or his dogs when Tilda climbed down the ladder into the room below, but there was a loaf of bread and some jam out on the table.

"Help yourself," Duska said. "And then come out to the cart."

A few minutes later, Tilda walked out of the cabin, chewing on her breakfast. Benji was backing an ancient-looking pony between the shafts of a weathered cart while Oak and Flame looked on. The pony stamped and snickered as Tilda approached.

Isaak was making sure the luggage was secure and Duska was already sitting up on the box seat.

"You'll have to be in the back," Isaak called as he climbed up beside Duska and took hold of the reins.

With her bread and jam clamped between her teeth to keep her hands free, Tilda hauled herself up and squeezed into a space between the trunks and bags.

Benji came to stand beside Duska. "You take care, Lady. 'Specially if you find yourself having to go down any mines."

Duska leant down and rested a hand on the Door Keeper's shoulder, where he covered it with his own. "You know I will avoid that, unless I absolutely have to."

Benji patted Duska's hand and stepped back. "Off you go, then."

"All set?" Isaak asked over his shoulder. Then he gave the reins a flick to encourage the pony, and the cart rattled away from the clearing.

Still trying to eat, Tilda was jolted and bumped against the trunks. By the time she'd finished, there was more jam around her mouth than in it, she felt bruised and battered, and they'd only driven a few miles. Duska had said it was going to take half a day to reach the town—how many more bruises would Tilda have by then? She squirmed and fidgeted, until she managed to wedge herself more securely in the space and, having made herself more comfortable, decided to find out more about the place they were going to.

"What's Digdown like?"

"Busy. Full of miners, like you'd expect."

Tilda huffed. She could have guessed that. "Are the mines close to town?"

"Reasonably."

Duska usually had more to say than this. Tilda twisted round to look at her; Duska's back was ramrod straight. She seemed awfully tense . . . And then Tilda remembered what Duska had said to Benji as they left. "Will *we* have to go into the mines?"

The look that flashed between Isaak and Duska spoke volumes.

"You may as well tell her before we get there," Isaak muttered.

Duska sighed and her body relaxed a little. "Tilda, I am hoping very much that I will not have to go into any mines. I'm terrified of being underground, you see." She gave a little laugh.

What in Power was funny about that?

"I wasn't always scared. When I was a child, my brothers and I used to play quite happily in the entrances to the tunnels and pretend to be miners. I'd imagine finding the biggest, rarest gems . . ." Duska paused. "Problem was, there was one time when I found a real one. It was a chance in a million, had probably slipped out of a miner's pocket, but I picked up a real rosario. My brothers were so angry at my luck, they devised what they felt was a fitting punishment."

Tilda almost regretted having to ask. "What did they do?"

"We went further into the tunnels than we'd ever gone before. And then they blew out my candle, turned and ran, leaving me in the dark." Duska shivered violently, making the cart tremble. "Our father—a miner himself—came to find me when the boys admitted what they'd done. Ever since, I have been afraid to go into the mines unless it is with a guide and extremely well lit. And even then, I cannot be there long before the panic rises in me."

Power. Poor Duska. No wonder she was looking for a Master to help them.

Tilda turned away and stared down the track. "Do the other mages know?"

"Only Silviu. And now you."

Tears prickled Tilda's eyes. "Thank you for trusting me."

Isaak snapped the reins and the cart trundled onwards. Eventually, after several long hours of nothing but trees to look at, they turned off the narrow track onto a more defined, well used one.

"We've still some way to go until we hit the town," Duska announced. "But you'll start to see some of the miner's homes. They are forced to live out here, because more unscrupulous Masters don't provide lodgings for their teams."

Tilda stared at two lopsided and patched tents pitched beside the track, a washing line full of shirts strung between them. A rickety tripod hung over cold ashes nearby. Benji's simple cabin was luxurious, compared to these.

There were more tents as Isaak drove the cart on, and then— huddled together in clearings either natural or man-made—some simple huts. The huts began to outnumber the tents as the track became a definite road.

Isaak guided the cart around a corner and quite suddenly there were no more trees. "Welcome to Digdown."

Tilda twisted round and knelt up to look. Her mouth dropped open.

They were definitely in a town now. On either side of the long road, two- and three-storey buildings stretched away into the distance, each one built within spitting distance of its neighbour. Every now and again, a narrow side street forced the buildings further apart, and from these openings poured a stream of men.

"Where are they all coming from?" Tilda gasped. "And where are they going?"

Most of the men wore a kind of uniform; stiff leather trousers tucked into heavy calf-high boots, a padded leather jerkin worn over a plain coloured shirt, and a helmet. Every grimy face was turned in the same direction: into town.

"From the mines," Duska said. "Shift's over, so they're on the way home or going to the bath houses, via Main Street. They always finish earlier the day before Weighing, and a few must've already washed up. See them?"

Tilda did, because there was a second uniform, although very few were wearing it yet; a dark jacket, crisp white shirt, long dark trousers, shiny shoes, and a glowing face.

The more Tilda looked at the crowds walking alongside the cart, the more she realised something was missing. "There aren't any women."

"Oh, there'll be some." Isaak had slowed the cart to a walking pace. "Not many are miners. Most of the women you find here are team mothers or bathkeepers. Others run shops and laundries, or entertain—"

"Here's our turning, Isaak," Duska said.

"Ho, turning right," Isaak shouted. "Turning right!"

The miners to the right of the cart hung back, creating a gap big enough for Isaak to make the turn. There were fewer miners walking here, so Tilda looked at the buildings instead. They were crammed as tightly together as out on Main Street, with some of them advertising lodgings or private wash rooms.

Isaak hauled on the reins and drew the cart to a halt outside the only house in the street with a pot of flowers beside the door.

Duska jumped down. "At last."

"This is your house?" Tilda stared up at the crooked beams and tiny windows as she scrambled down from the cart. It didn't look like the kind of house a powermage would live in.

"I like things simpler when I'm in my home region." Duska pulled on the chain hanging beside the door, and somewhere deep inside the house, a bell rang.

A woman who was in the middle of a good grumble opened the door. "—keep trying to get this floor scrubbed, but no, I keep getting interrupted. Yes?" She frowned at Tilda.

Duska burst out laughing. "Power bless you, Sasha."

The woman's eyes flicked towards her and widened. "My Lady! I wasn't expect—! I was trying to—!" She threw her hands up into the air. "Oh, Power!"

Duska pulled the flustered woman into a hug. "It's good to see you, too, Sasha."

Sasha wriggled free, looking worried. "If I'd known you were coming, I'd have scrubbed faster. Well, come in, come in." She backed into the house, talking all the while. "Just mind the bucket and step round that wet patch. I'd have bought a chook if I'd known you'd be here for dinner."

"After you, Tilda," Duska said.

Following the sound of Sasha's voice, Tilda stepped inside. She avoided a bucket of soapy water, stepped carefully over the still-wet floor, and found Sasha pulling dust covers off the chairs in a large, bright sitting room.

"I'd have done this sooner if I'd known. Sit yourselves down, now. Do you want anything to eat or drink? Are you here long? And who's this new face, then?"

Did this woman ever draw breath? Which question should Tilda answer first?

"We had breakfast on the way, we're here for the foreseeable future, and this"—Duska put an arm around Tilda's shoulder—"is Matilda, the new Mage of Merjan."

"Mage of Merjan is she?" Sasha tilted her head. "Ah, but there's a touch of Pergatt there, if I'm not mistaken? Something about the eyes . . ."

Tilda's green eyes prickled as she nodded. "My Pa always said a true Pergattian's eyes were green from the trees, and his hair red from the earth. I only ended up with the tree bit, really. He is . . . was . . . from Pergatt."

"Was? Ohhh . . . you poor mite."

Tilda blinked hard, chewed her lip to stop it wobbling, and was spared the need to respond.

"Well, I know we've only just arrived," Duska said, "but how about we leave Isaak to bring our luggage in, Sasha to finish the floor, and take ourselves off for a walk into town so you can get a feel for the place, Tilda? I'd like to make sure a certain Master is available to see me tomorrow."

"It's Weighing, so he should be," Sasha said. "Tell you what, why don't you bring me a chook for dinner, too? Saves me going out and leaving this floor mucky."

By the time Tilda and Duska retraced their steps, Main Street was even busier than when they'd left it. Hundreds of men stomped up and down the elevated wooden walkways, which had been built along the fronts of shops, hotels, and bars. Some of the men were still covered in dust and grime from their day's work, but many more were now as clean and bright as a new pin. A few of them eyed Tilda and Duska with passing interest, but there were no pointing fingers or curious stares here. Not even a respectful bow. No one here would know who Tilda was of course, but surely some of them recognised Duska?

"Do they know who you are?" Tilda asked.

"Not really. I don't usually advertise my presence in Digdown unless I'm here on official business."

"But you are. Aren't you?"

Duska glanced down at Tilda. "Official business may be conducted out in the open, or not."

"And we're . . . not?"

"That's right. Now, here's where we're going to find our dinner."

At first sight, Arker's Food Store was no different to any food shop Tilda had been to in Merjan City. Covered barrels of flour, rice, and sugar were lined up with military precision on the wooden walkway outside, while inside, there was a cabinet for fresh meat and cheese, and shelves packed with all manner of tins and jars and packets. The only difference was that Arker's also sold anything edible that could be dried, salted, or pickled and still make a good meal. Including, Tilda was revolted to see, bags of dried worms.

"I've got the chicken," Duska said, holding up a brown-paper-and-string wrapped parcel. "Let's go and see what else we can find, shall we?"

The smell of fresh-baked meat pies wafting out of Vendra's Victuals set Tilda's stomach rumbling. And not just hers, it seemed; a still-dusty miner was inspecting the golden-crusted pies piled high in the window.

"One of them'd do me right," he muttered and stared at the coin he was holding. Then he sighed and turned to walk away.

Tilda watched him go. "If he wanted a pie, why didn't he go in?"

"Didn't you see the sign?" Duska pointed.

"No unwashed. Oh."

They continued to stroll along the walkway, dodging between the miners, Tilda pestering Duska with questions about the various shops and buildings at almost every other step.

"The Exchange? Well, that's where the Masters trade in their stones. And the miners too, if they are independent and don't work for a Master." Duska stepped around a group of men who'd stopped to chat. "There's many an ounce of glimmer changes hands in there."

Tilda frowned as she ducked under a miner's arm. "Glimmer?"

Duska nodded. "Miners have a currency of their own. Glimmer's made up of the smallest pieces of stone which the gemsmen don't like using. It's usually saved up until there's at least an ounce in weight. An ounce of glimmer's worth ten bits. There are twenty bits to a circoin and ten circoins to a mark."

They were passing Trumat's Tools. Outside was a rack of picks and shovels, each with a price label attached. "So . . . that spade could be bought for five bits or half an ounce of glimmer?"

"Exactly. Although you have to trade in your glimmer for hard coin first. No merchant will spend time weighing out glimmer."

Tilda frowned again, trying to get to grips with the idea of a whole new currency. "Why bother with glimmer then, if it's too small for the gemsmen to use?"

"The largest pieces might be used to make cheap jewellery. The rest is often ground up and added to resin to coat wood or metal and give it a bit of sparkle. Certain stones are also used by the Medicians in their medicines—the tiniest pieces are crushed so fine, the powder can be added to food or drink."

Next to Trumat's, the brass handled doors of The Miner's Mansion stood open. Tilda peered inside and saw a guest taking possession of keys from the manager behind the desk. Walking on, she smelt Hoker's Livery long before she reached it; there were few horses in the stables but plenty of mules, all chewing contentedly at bundles of straw. The windows of The Dirty Shovel were masked by lacy drapes, but they couldn't mask the sound of laughter and the chink of glasses from within.

Duska's face darkened as she passed quickly by it. "There are too many taverns in Digdown. And it looks as though there's yet another opened since I was last here."

As Tilda drew level with The Digger's Delight, a dirty young man fell out of the door and landed at her feet. A woman burst out of the door after him; she was shaking her fist.

"Don't you come back 'til you're clean!" she shrieked. "I'll not 'ave unwashed in my establishment!"

The youth leapt up and ran his hands through his hair, releasing a cloud of red dust into the air. "Aww, Millie Mae! 'Twas only a bit o' fun. Won't you forgive me? I've a pouchful o' glimmer, an' I'm minded to wager it. Don' make me drink it in The Dirty Shovel instead."

The woman pursed her lips. "A pouchful of glimmer, eh?"

The youth nodded. "That's right."

"Well, you come back when you're scrubbed up and you've traded that glimmer for hard coin, and I might just let you back in."

The youth grinned and scampered away.

The woman saw Duska and Tilda watching. "What? Tis only a card game or two." She sniffed and went back inside.

"So now we have gambling dens as well. The regulations have been relaxed too far . . ." Duska shook her head.

Tilda wasn't listening. She'd caught sight of another gemsman's shop and hurried over to look. She pressed so close to the glass, it misted with her breath.

How many pedestals were in this window? Tilda lost count and took a guess. Fifty? A hundred? She didn't know where to look first. Variously sized stones perched on top of the pedestals, grouped according to colour. Some were cut and polished into dazzling brilliants, others remained rough and unprocessed, disguising their potential beauty.

"Ah, Gemsman Rayn Bow. One of the best, and the only one in Digdown would you believe," Duska said, joining Tilda at the window. "The majority of gemsmen live and work in Jewlton, where it's cleaner and there's a better class of customer. Rayn prefers to live and work here. Says he gets the pick of the stones, working this close to the mines, and I have to say he always has unusual or top quality gems. Lovely, aren't they?"

"Beautiful," Tilda breathed.

She was vaguely aware of Duska saying something about going inside to check the price of a firestone, and mumbled a reply, too caught up gazing at the display to answer properly. She recognized the green pergatts—Duska often had them sewn to her gowns— but she'd never even heard of blue aquarts. The firestone Duska had expressed an interest in was present in every shade of red and orange—and sometimes both in the same stone. And then there were purple nargants, pink rosarios, snowstones, limonaes, quertz—

"It'll be me first in the tub, Sparkles!" someone shouted, pounding past Tilda.

Startled, she stepped away from the window and spun round, right into the middle of the walkway.

"Watch out!"

"Oof!"

A filthy miner crashed into Tilda and sent her sprawling in a cloud of dust. She choked and coughed as the young man leapt to his feet.

"Dammit, Yanni," he yelled. "It was my turn tonight!"

A whoop of triumph came from further down the road as Tilda managed to catch her breath and climb shakily to her feet. "I'm fine. Thanks for asking."

The miner rounded on her. "You should look where you're going." He snatched up a bag from the walkway.

Anger heated Tilda's cheeks. "And you should *walk* on the pavement, not run," she snapped, glaring at him.

"You'd run too, if you were me. That hot water should be mine," he snarled, then ran off after the long gone Yanni.

Duska hurried out of the shop. "Tilda, are you alright? I saw what happened."

"Yes. Apart from being covered in this muck." She tried to brush the worst of the dust off. "He barged straight into me, and all for some hot water."

"Ah . . ." To Tilda's surprise, Duska laughed. "You don't want to get between a miner and his after shift bath. I've seen grown men fight over who's next into the tub. They have races sometimes, you know, see who can get down and cleaned up the quickest."

"I'll make sure I'm out of their way next time." To Tilda's embarassment, she felt her bottom lip tremble.

Duska must've noticed; she put a hand on Tilda's shoulder. "I think it might be best if we find Feliks tomorrow. Shall we go back? See if Sasha's finished washing that floor yet so she can get this chook cooked?"

Tilda nodded gratefully and looked down the road; the miner who'd crashed into her was just turning the corner. "I hope your bath water's cold when you get in it," she muttered under her breath.

Chapter 9

The Weighing

"THE WEIGHING IS held weekly," Duska told Tilda the following day, when they returned to Main Street. "Every Master attends to oversee the finds of their teams. The finds are weighed and credited, and then the miners get paid. It's the only day they don't work. There's always a lot of interest in how well rival teams have done. It gets very competitive."

The men on Main Street were all heading in the same direction again, except this time it wasn't the bathhouses they were aiming for. Everyone was already clean, and they were all moving towards a huge two storey building sitting at the farthest end of the road like a full stop in a sentence. Above and across the width of four sets of double doors in the front of the building was a large sign.

"The Weighspace," Tilda read.

"Just so. We'll go in and watch the Weighing, then I'll find Feliks." Duska took hold of Tilda's shoulders. "Now, remember what I said. Try not to draw attention to yourself."

Apart from the fact that they were females in a colossal crowd of men, Tilda didn't think anyone would take too much notice of them; Duska had insisted that they both wore dark trousers with dark jackets over white shirts. At first glance, they probably looked like off duty miners.

"I'll be as unnoticeable as I can," she told Duska.

Inside the Weighspace, the rumble of men's voices was incredibly loud. Was the entire population of Digdown in this one enormous room? Men were everywhere; some sat at tables and were involved in card games, others stood in groups, talking. There was a wide range of ages; boys who looked to be not much older than Tilda, pimpled youths, swaggering young men, middle aged fellows wiry from hard labour, and even the odd grey haired elder. There *were* women, but they were few and far between and, like the men, were dressed in what Tilda now thought of as off-duty uniform.

Today though, something new had been added to that uniform; every single miner had a coloured neckerchief tied around his or her throat. Tilda's throat felt terribly bare when she realised.

"This way, Tilda." Duska moved easily through the thickening crowd towards a wide raised platform.

Tilda followed close, glancing around. The coloured neckers seemed to be a code of some sort, because miners wearing the same colour tended to be standing together. And the necker colours affected the miners behaviour, too; those miners wearing red around their throats exchanged smiles with those wearing blue, but ignored those wearing striped black and white. And miners with orange and white striped neckers scowled openly and occasionally shook fists at those wearing purple.

"This will do." Duska stopped. "Can you see from here?"

She could. They were standing to the front and left of the room, near a short flight of steps leading up onto the platform. There was a matching set of steps on the other side and various well-dressed men and women were climbing up both. A row of chairs lined the platform.

"They're the Masters," Duska said. "Can you see they wear their team colours?"

So that's what the coloured neckers were—a way of identifying different Masters' teams. All but one of the Masters were wearing them too. Tilda pointed at a short fellow, his throat as bare as her own, sitting at a desk on which rested a large ledger, a bell, and a pair of scales. "He isn't."

"That's because Donalt's not a Master. He's the Weigher. An impartial judge of quality, employed jointly by all the Masters so they are assured of fair treatment and accurate prices."

Donalt picked up the bell and rang it three times. The crowd surged towards the platform, some of the teams jostling and pushing others, as the Masters took their seats. One chair remained empty.

Heads turned, looking for something—or perhaps someone?

"Might've known Feliks'd be the last in again," a grizzled miner growled, right behind Tilda.

Feliks? Wasn't that the Master Duska wanted to meet? If he didn't come, they were off to a bad start indeed. Tilda chewed her lip and craned her neck to look for him, even though she didn't know who she was looking for.

A few more of the men standing nearby muttered among themselves.

"He knows we can't start 'til all the Masters arrive."

"He's never missed a Weighing yet."

"Will he have another white velvet?"

"He's here!" someone called.

There was a movement in the mass of miners, and they parted to let someone through. Tilda stood on tiptoes to see.

Among the dark jackets of the miners, this late arrival stood out like a peacock among crows. His trousers and jacket were light grey, but instead of a coloured necker, his waistcoat, cravat—even the band of ribbon around his tall hat—were different shades of turquoise. A cheer rose up from a small group of miners wearing turquoise neckers, and the newcomer acknowledged them with a wave.

"Blasted show off," a disgruntled miner muttered.

"About time, Feliks Weaverson."

Feliks grinned at the woman who'd addressed him from her seat on the platform. Sweeping the hat from his head, he bowed low. "Rosa, my love. How lovely you look today." He straightened with a gleam in his eye. "Are you eager to see what my boys have found this month?"

"I'm hoping they've left something decent for the rest of us," Rosa snapped, her cheeks as pink as the necker she wore. "Just sit down, will you?"

Feliks took the steps to the stage two at a time and threw himself down in the one remaining chair. He crossed his legs, fetched a slim silver case from his inside pocket, and removed a dark cigar, which he stuck between his lips.

"No smoking," Rosa hissed.

"I wasn't going to." But Feliks kept the cigar clamped between his teeth and leaned back in the chair. "Shall we begin?"

Donalt consulted a parchment, and shouted, "Master Redwein."

From among the Masters, a short, stocky fellow with a purple necker rose to his feet.

"Team leader, Erik Grit."

A miner in a matching necker leapt onto the platform and handed over a leather pouch.

"The team leaders carry the pouches which contain their team's finds from the working week," Duska said quietly. "Donalt will announce the contents, decide how much the finds are worth, and the Master will pay the teams accordingly once he's traded the stones for coin."

Donalt tipped the contents of the pouch onto his table. After a brief inspection, he wrote something on the parchment. "Two ounces of glimmer and three dozen rosarios."

Another name was called, another purple-neckered miner climbed onto the stage, and another inspection was made. Tilda counted how many team leaders went up with purple neckers— five—before another Master, with a red necker, was called up with his team leaders for the accounting.

As Donalt called out the various finds for the week, there was cheering and backslapping and handshaking for those with good finds, and happy looking Masters. But there were frowns and fist

shaking and grumbling for those who weren't so fortunate, which
seemed to include the grizzled miner standing behind Tilda.

"We need a break in our luck," he grumbled. "It's that damned
new chipper, I told him he'd cut 'em too small. Keep 'em big, I said,
they're worth more that way, but would he listen?"

Tilda tugged Duska's sleeve. "Rosa looks happy."

Duska nodded. "She does. That last team must've tapped the end
of a seam to have found so many firestones. I hope they've got that
particular tunnel well marked, or the other Masters will be all over
it when the next shift starts."

Before Tilda could ask what tapping a seam or marking meant,
Donalt called for Feliks Weaverson and Nicolo Tarant.

From the crowd came catcalls and shouts.

"What've you got this time, Sparkles?"

"Hope it's nowt more than a pouchful of glimmer. 'Bout time
Feliks left some of the good stuff for the rest of us."

Everyone seemed to be jostling for a better position; a large
miner stepped right in front of Tilda, blocking her view. She tried to
push round him, but was pinned so tightly by other men pressing
forward, she could barely move. All she could do was listen.

As the men quietened down, Tilda heard the hollow echo of
someone walking across the platform. There was a moment of
silence, then a rattle. That must be the stones being tipped out for
Donalt to inspect. There was a clink or two of weights being placed
on the scales, more silence and then—

"Four ounces of glimmer and a baker's dozen of limones," Donalt
announced.

Laughter broke out in the crowd.

"Did you and yer boys sleep most of yer shifts, Nico?"

"Pretty poor show, Feliks."

"Oh, we were wide awake," someone shouted. "Show 'em what
else we found, Nico!"

In an instant, the mood in the room changed. Tension crackled,
almost Power-like, as around Tilda, men started to mutter.

"White velvet."

"He's got another velvet!"

"Are you sure?"

What was a white velvet? Determined to see, Tilda wriggled and squeezed past the big miner, but could get no further forward. Through gaps in the tightly packed crowd, she caught a glimpse of Feliks standing beside Donalt's table; of a miner whose face she couldn't see, handing a small bundle of white fabric over; and of Donalt, eyebrows raised as he opened the fabric.

The room fell silent, and a miner in front of Tilda moved, blocking her view. Suddenly she heard a burst of music, very faint and fading fast. Then the miner moved and she could see again.

Donalt's face was pale when he looked up from his inspection. "It's dragon's eye."

In an explosion of sound, the miners surged towards the platform, some cheering, others yelling angrily. Squashed as she was between some of them, Tilda was carried forward too, until Duska grabbed her arm and held on tight.

"We should get out of here," Duska shouted above the noise. "This could get messy."

Pushing back against the pressure of the surge, they finally broke free of the mass. Tilda couldn't see the platform or what was happening anymore, but she could finally speak without shouting. "What's so special about a . . . a dragon's eye?"

"It's very rare. And often a pointer to other rare stones, too. There'll be some argument now over where it was found, whether any other teams had prior claim to the tunnels, how long to allow Feliks access to the site before the exclusivity is lost." She looked round at the nearest miners. "Now, what I need is . . . Ah, there's one. Ho! You!"

Standing at the edge of the crowd was a young miner with a turquoise necker. He looked left and right, then pointed at his chest. "Me?"

"Yes, you." Duska beckoned him over. "Tell your Master I have some business I'd like to discuss with him."

To Tilda's astonishment, the miner simply looked Duska up and down. "You'd do better going to a gemsman, missis. Feliks don't do business direct."

Duska smiled. It wasn't a nice smile.

The young man took a step back.

"He will do business direct with me. Tell him to expect a visitor at his office within the hour."

The miner blinked, nodded, and pushed and shoved his way back through the crowd.

"Let's go," Duska said as the miner disappeared with a last flash of turquoise. "We'll spend a little time window shopping, I think. Give Feliks a chance to get to his office before we do."

Chapter 10

A Plan Takes Shape

EXACTLY AN HOUR later, Tilda and Duska were shown into Feliks' office.

The first thing Tilda saw was the man himself, sitting behind a large desk.

"Mam, miss, welcome. Please, sit." Feliks stood up and walked round the desk to greet his visitors properly, gesturing towards a couch. He'd taken off his jacket, and the turquoise of his waistcoat seemed brighter than ever.

"Thank you." Duska took a seat and indicated that Tilda should sit next to her.

The inky-fingered man who'd shown the mages into the office sat himself at a second, much smaller desk in a corner. He pulled a piece of paper towards him, picked up a pen, and looked up expectantly.

Feliks remained standing. He smiled. "It is rather unusual to deal directly with a Master, but I believe you have some business to discuss with me? My secretary will take notes."

"No, he will not." Duska crossed her legs and leaned back on the couch. "The discussion is for your ears only, Feliks Weaverson."

Surprise flashed across Feliks' face, but he hid it quickly and studied his guests.

Tilda tried not to squirm.

As though he'd come to a decision, Feliks gave a quick nod and turned towards the other man. "Arter, would you be so kind to bring refreshments for my guests and see that we're not disturbed?"

The little man screwed his face into a tight smile, lay down his pen, and stood up. "Of course." He slammed the door on the way out.

Tilda jumped. It seemed that Arter wasn't used to being excluded from the Master's meetings.

Feliks leaned against his desk, and crossed his arms. "You obviously know who I am, but would you care to introduce yourself, mam?"

Duska smiled. "I am Lady Duska, Mage of Pergatt."

For a second time, Feliks almost managed to hide his surprise. He inclined his head. "I am honoured, my Lady. And your maid's name?"

"I'm not a maid." Tilda looked at Duska, who raised a single eyebrow at her and said nothing. It was obvious that Tilda was going to have to speak for herself here. She took a deep breath. "I'm the Lady Matilda, Mage of Merjan."

This time Feliks couldn't hide his surprise at all; his eyes widened and flicked between his guests, his mouth opening and closing as though he was searching for words.

The office door opened, and Arter entered with a tray on which a carafe of dark red liquid and three empty glasses sat. He set the tray down on his desk and picked up the carafe. "Shall I pour?"

"Thank you, Arter, but I'll do that," Feliks said, finally finding his voice. "You may leave us."

Arter banged the carafe down and scowled at Tilda as he left.

Why was he—Did he think she was a maid, too? That she was shirking her duties? Wait until he found out she was a powermage.

While Feliks poured the cordial, Duska pointed at the door and muttered something Tilda didn't quite catch. There was a brief flash of green around the door's edge.

"I didn't think we were supposed to be using our Power unless we absolutely needed to," Tilda whispered.

"But I don't want anyone listening in," Duska whispered back. "It didn't take much."

"The frazerberry cordial is quite refreshing," Feliks said, offering Tilda the first glass. "My apologies, Lady Matilda, for the assumption. I hope you can forgive me?"

Tilda took the glass and nodded. It was still so strange to hear herself being called Lady Matilda. Would she ever get used to it, she wondered, and took a sip of her drink. It tasted of summer.

"So. Power bless our business." Feliks handed Duska a second glass and raised his own in a toast before sitting behind his desk again. "What can I do for you, my Ladies?"

Duska ran her finger around the rim of her glass. "Has news reached Pergatt of certain . . . difficulties, experienced at Ring Isle a short while ago?"

Feliks nodded. "I had heard something. Details were a little sketchy."

"All you need to know is that as a result, there is an issue with the Ringstone. Some damage."

"Oh?" Feliks' glass halted, half way to his mouth. "And you need me because . . . ?"

"Your team has one of the best records when it comes to mining the rarest of stones. We are hoping that you will loan them to us and allow them to work for us. At least until we find what we are looking for."

"I see." Feliks leaned forward and set his glass down carefully. "And you cannot find it yourselves?"

"No."

Tilda held her breath. Was Duska going to admit that she couldn't bear to go into the mines herself?

It seemed not. When Duska did not explain further, Feliks rubbed his chin thoughtfully. "Which stone do you need to find?"

"It's not a stone we need." Duska took a deep breath. "To make the repair, we need silviron."

For five heartbeats—Tilda counted them—Feliks just stared at Duska. Then he burst out laughing.

How dare he? Anger bubbled up in Tilda's stomach. "Stop laughing!" she snapped, more sharply than she'd intended. "It's not a joke."

Feliks choked off his laughter. "I'm sorry, I meant no offence, but . . . silviron? It has not been mined since—"

"The first powermages were initiated. Yes, we know." Tilda set her glass down. "But there's more of it."

"Really?" Feliks looked at Duska. "Where?"

"Do you mind? The Power told me, not Lady Duska." Seeing the warning look Duska shot at her, Tilda took a calming breath. She wouldn't get very far if she took offence every time someone consulted an adult mage and ignored her, would she? People weren't expecting to take instruction or receive information from a child. She had to remember that. "Where it was found before."

Feliks turned his head slowly and looked at her. "Somewhere in the oldest mines, then. And—?"

"That's all we know," she admitted.

"I see." Feliks rubbed his chin again. "And you're asking for my team's help to find it?"

"If your team can find dragon's eye, I'm hoping they might also find something as rare as silviron." Duska leaned forward. "But none of them must know what it is they are mining for until they find it."

Feliks spread his arms wide. "How will we explain that? It'll be obvious something's going on when I ask the team to start digging in a place where no one's mined for years. Especially after the dragon's eye. Questions would be asked about why we'd left that tunnel after such a discovery."

He was right, they would.

Tilda frowned. They had to be able to explain to other mining teams in Digdown why such an unusual event was occurring. Feliks' team needed a good reason, a *believable* reason, to explain leaving their current site and moving nearer to where the first and only hoard of silviron had been mined.

And then Tilda had an idea. "Use me!"

Duska frowned. "What do you mean?"

Tilda jumped to her feet and paced up and down, the words tumbling from her lips almost as fast as she was thinking them. "We can hide this in plain sight. I'm a new powermage, got lots to learn about the history of powermaging and the regions. Why don't we tell everyone we're here so I can see where the silviron was mined from, and to learn about mining stones and gems because that's what Pergatt's famous for. We can say we were at the Weighing to . . ." She paused in her pacing just long enough for inspiration to strike again. "To work out which of the Masters and teams we thought deserved the honour of teaching me about mining. And after the dragon's eye find, surely no one would question us asking you?" Out of breath, she stopped and looked at Feliks.

"That's not a bad idea." He pushed his chair back, rose slowly, and walked around the desk. "Not a bad idea at all. The other Masters won't like it of course, having missed out on such an honour, but they'd believe it."

"There you go." Excitement bubbled in Tilda's chest and she spun round. "Duska, what do you think?"

Duska was frowning. "Tilda, mining's hard work and you don't know the first thing about—" She turned to Feliks. "We can't send Lady Matilda down the mines. She's a mage, for Power's sake! What if there was gas. Or a rockfall? Or she got lost in the tunnels?" She turned to Tilda and her voice dropped to a whisper. "What if you feel the same way about the darkness as me?"

"I'm not afraid of the dark," Tilda said. Which was true, up to a point. She'd never been in a mine before to find out.

Feliks sat on the edge of his desk and crossed his arms. "Lady Duska, you said yourself my team has a reputation. Nico's one of the best team leaders in Digdown. Good at finding stones and hasn't lost a teammate in all the time he's been leader. Lady Matilda will be safe with him, I can assure you."

"Please, Duska? I will be careful. Please, let me do this," Tilda begged. "It's the only way we'll be able to justify being here, and who knows, I might actually be useful to the team." She held her breath, waiting for Duska's response.

"It might work," Duska finally admitted.

Tilda let her breath out in a great whoosh of relief and sat back down on the couch, grinning. It would work, she was certain of it. She'd found something she could do, which relied on her being a new powermage, rather than being unable to do anything because of the same thing.

"I won't let you down," she promised.

Feliks strode over to the door and flung it open. "Arter! Find Nico, and get him here. Fast."

Ten minutes later, there was a knock on the door.

"Come," Feliks called.

A young man poked his head round the door. As soon as she saw his face, Tilda went hot, then cold. Oh Power, this couldn't be Nico . . . could it?

It seemed it could.

Feliks beckoned the young man in. "Nico, good of you to get here so quickly. A nice stone your team handed in today, very nice. Come in, shut the door."

"Thanks." Nico stayed close to the door. "I don't want to waste the rest of my day off, Feliks, so what d'you want?"

"It's not me who needs you. It's them." Feliks pointed at the couch.

Nico followed the finger and seemed to realise for the first time that Feliks had guests. "Mam," he said to Duska, and then looked at Tilda. "Miss . . . oh." He frowned. "It's you."

Feliks looked from Nico to Tilda and back again. "You've already met?"

"You could say that," Tilda muttered.

Duska laid a hand on Tilda's knee and squeezed it gently. "Allow me to introduce ourselves, Nico. I am the Lady Duska of Pergatt, and this—"

"Is Lady Matilda of Merjan," Tilda finished for her.

"Powermages? She's a . . ." Nico took a moment to collect himself. "Then I'm really sorry about yesterday, I—"

He *should* be sorry. Tilda felt a stab of satisfaction at his discomfort, but decided to be gracious—they needed him too much. "Apology accepted."

"You're not here because of that incident, though," Duska began. "The Lady Matilda—"

Tilda sat up a little straighter and tried to look more mage-y. It wouldn't do any harm to remind him of her position.

"—as a newly initiated mage," Duska continued, "needs to learn about Issraya's history and the peculiarities of regions other than her own. As I was due to make a trip home, I've brought her with me to find out about Pergattian mining and to see where the Ringstone's silviron came from. I was impressed by your most recent find, and Feliks has kindly agreed to allow Lady Matilda to accompany your team into the old mines as part of her education."

"An honour, don't you think?" Feliks smoothed his waistcoat front. "To be chosen over all the other teams?"

"It might well be an honour, but you won't make much money from us while we're babysitting," Nico stated bluntly, the frown back on his face. "Even if we let her play at digging, those mines are pretty empty of stones."

"All of you will be suitably repaid for your time," Duska said.

That did nothing to smooth the frown from Nico's brow. "I don't have a choice, then, do I?"

"No. Lady Matilda will be part of your team from tomorrow." Feliks' lips were a thin, tight line.

"Huh." Nico reached for the door handle. "She stopping in the team house, too?"

Team house? Tilda had no idea what that was, but if she was going to make this lie work, she had to pretend there was nothing she wanted more than to learn everything there was to know about mining life. Including team houses. "Of course."

"How long for?"

Tilda squared her shoulders. "As long as it takes. Depends how good a teacher you are."

Nico's lip curled and he pulled the door open. "Then make sure you're at Gerty Grunback's in Paradise Street, six bells tomorrow morning, my Lady. I'll teach you mining. Every little bit of it, if that's what you want."

"It is," Tilda managed to say before Nico slammed the door behind him. Then she pasted a smile on her face for Duska and Feliks, but inside she was shaking.

What in Power's name had she got herself into?

Chapter 11

The Miner Mage

A LITTLE BEFORE six bells the next morning, Tilda and Duska turned onto Paradise Street.

"It doesn't really live up to its name, does it?" Tilda hefted her bag higher onto her shoulder and eyed up the houses either side of the narrow street. There was barely enough room for three people to walk side by side down here, and if you had long legs, you'd probably be able to cross the street by stepping from one overhanging balcony to another.

"Maybe not, but it's home to many of the miners, and might well seem like paradise compared to where some of them might have been housed before," Duska said. "Remember the tents?"

Tilda nodded.

"There are several team houses down here. See the double doors?"

Tilda looked. Nearly every house front had not one, but two doors in it; one door was always brightly painted, the other was simply varnished wood. "Why two?"

"One clean, one dirty. Going to or returning from shift, the miners use the plain door. If they're washed up and are off duty, they go in and out of the painted one. The colour will tell you which Master's team lives there.

That meant they were looking for a turquoise door. Tilda passed an orange one, a green, and then she saw it. "That one?" She tugged at the chain hanging between the two doors. A bell rang inside the house; before it had stopped jangling, the unpainted door was opened by Nico.

Duska smiled. "Good morning, Nico."

"My Lady." Nico stepped aside to let her enter.

"Oh, I'm not coming in," Duska said.

Tilda spun round to look at her. "You're not?"

"No. I think from here on in, you're best on your own. It's going to be difficult enough for Nico to have to explain your presence to his team without having me around to complicate things." Duska raised a hand, almost like a blessing. "Power be with you, Tilda. I will see you at the next Weighing. Send word if you need me before then."

The next Weighing? That meant she would be on her own for a whole week. Tilda gulped. Except she wouldn't be on her own, would she? She'd be with the rest of Nico's team. "I won't let you down," she murmured.

"I'm sure you won't." Duska gave Tilda a reassuring smile and looked at Nico. "Take care of her, Nico."

"Yes, Lady. Come on in, then."

Tilda stepped into the team house and glanced over her shoulder; she had just enough time to register Duska's concerned expression before Nico closed the door and shut her out. Tilda's heart jolted in her chest. She was properly on her own now. Finding the silviron was up to her—and how she managed to use this team of miners.

"Right. Let's get you kitted out. You've come in the mud, or dirty entrance," Nico told Tilda as she followed him along a narrow corridor with bare wood floors.

"But I'm not dirty. Or muddy."

"Not yet, you're not. But I'm in my work gear, so I have to use this side. In here." Nico opened a door to his right. "This is where we get changed. Each team member has their own box."

The boxes were small cubicles with doors, built around the walls of the room. Each cubicle had a short bench and two shelves inside it; under every bench was a pair of heavy boots, and on the shelves lay folded clothes.

"Off duty clean stuff goes on the top shelf, clean work gear next down, dirty gets dropped on the floor." Nico indicated one of the boxes. "That'll be yours. I've stuck some work gear in it, had to guess at the sizes, but I think you'll be right."

There was the sound of feet and voices in the corridor.

Nico gave Tilda a shove. "Get changed, quick. And don't come out 'til I tell you to."

She stepped into her box and Nico pulled its door shut, sealing her inside.

The voices and footsteps grew suddenly louder—the rest of the team must have arrived.

Nico raised his voice above the din. "Look lively, fellas. We need to be heading off soon."

"Did I hear the doorbell?" someone asked.

"Yes."

"So why are we . . . up earlier than normal, Sparkles?"

"And has it got owt to do with this being shut?"

Several sharp raps on Tilda's door made her jump.

"You'll find out soon enough, Yanni. Get yourself sorted first."

Either side of Tilda, doors banged shut, and then there was only the rustle of clothing and clomp of boots. She'd better get changed too. There were no clean clothes on her top shelf; she shoved her bag up there instead. She undressed quickly, her clothes joining the bag, and pulled on the "clean" work clothes that made up the uniform of a miner. The vest and shirt weren't too bad—they fitted, sort of. She only had to turn the sleeves back a little on the shirt to keep her hands free. The leather trousers were the stiffest, most uncomfortable things she'd ever worn on her legs. How did anyone walk in these? Let alone work. And as for the leather jerkin . . . She wrinkled her nose. It smelt of sweat and earth. She'd avoid wearing that until she had to. The other box doors started to bang open while she was still pulling on the calf-high boots.

"Right, everyone ready?"

Tilda's head shot up. Before she could shout "not yet" and finish tying her laces, Nico carried on talking.

"There's been a change of plan. We're not going back to where we found the dragon's eye."

"Eh?"

"You what?"

Tilda tied the knot on her second boot and perched on the edge of her bench, listening hard. Was this when Nico was going to tell his team about her . . . and about going to the old mines? Her stomach tightened. How would they react?

"The Lady Duska's in town. Asked Feliks if she could borrow us for a while."

"Duska? Powermage Duska?"

Tilda jumped. Was that a girl's voice?

"What's she want us for?"

And that was voice of the person who'd knocked on her door. Nico had called him Yanni. There was something familiar about the voice—could this possibly be Yanni, the bath-queue jumper?

"Bet she's after . . . a stone or two."

It would have been so much easier if stones were all that Duska wanted. Tilda chewed her lip, her head full of silviron.

"She's not after stones. She's after our expertise. Is paying us to teach someone about mining. Oh, stone in a swamp."

Two heavy blows landed on Tilda's door.

"You might as well come out," Nico called.

Tilda took a deep breath and stood up. Her hand shook as she opened the box door. There were five people standing outside, and all of them were staring at her.

She tried to smile. "Um. Hello."

"Another girl. At last." A young woman, her hair tied in two long plaits, grinned. "I'm Zander. And you are?"

"Team, meet Lady Matilda, Mage of Merjan," Nico said before Tilda could even open her mouth.

Zander's mouth fell open.

"*She's* a mage?"

Two miners had spoken at the same time. Tilda stared at the boys—tall, thick set, and so alike she could be forgiven for thinking she was seeing double. Twins.

Nico sighed and rolled his eyes. "Yes, she is."

"Sparkles, you're having a laugh."

So the bath-stealer *was* Yanni. Tilda recognised his voice. He was also the youth that Duska had ordered to give a message to Feliks at the Weighing.

Nico pointed at his face. "Do I look like I am? Lady Matilda here is going to be living and working with us until she thinks she's learnt enough about our jobs. Any questions?"

Four hands shot into the air.

"We'll walk and talk. Grab your bags and hats." Nico selected a helmet from a rack. "Better to wear your jerkin than carry it. It's easier," he told Tilda, then rammed the helmet onto her head.

"Ow!"

"Too big. Hand it back and try . . . this one."

Tilda snatched the second helmet from Nico before he had a chance to ram it on her head again. Thank Power this one fitted. No sooner had she put it on, than Nico thrust a rucsac at her, its contents jangling.

"Tools," Nico said, inspecting her. "You're good to go."

In the corridor outside the changing room an older woman waited, her fading auburn hair scraped back from her face and pulled into a tight, practical bun at the nape of her neck.

"Lunch," she said.

Each member of the team received a brown paper parcel and a bottle of water as they passed her.

"You must be Gerty," Tilda said when, last in the line, she accepted her lunch and water. She stuffed both into her bag and hoped the tools wouldn't squash the parcel too much.

"That I am, Lady. Team mother and house owner." Gerty smiled at her. "It's an honour to have you under my roof. Enjoy your first day."

"Thank you. See you later." Tilda hurried to catch up with the rest of the team.

Outside, Nico set off at a fast pace, leading them in silence through the narrow streets of Digdown. Tilda had expected to see a flood of miners again, this time heading out of town, but there were very few other teams around yet, and those she did see simply nodded or murmured a quiet greeting. Soon the town was left behind and she was climbing up into the forest along a narrow track.

Yanni fell into step beside her. "So why's a powermage got to learn about mining?"

Tilda pulled at her rucsac to make it sit more comfortably on her shoulders, giving herself time to think before she answered. It wouldn't do to give anything away this early on. "It's important that powermages know about all sorts of things. I'm not as old as mages usually are at their initiations, so I've got more to learn than most. I'm from Merjan, but here to learn all about Pergatt. Especially its history."

"What sort of history?" Zander had fallen into step on Tilda's other side.

"Um . . ." Tilda thought fast. How much should she tell them? Best stick to the facts. "Like where silviron was originally found."

Zander and Yanni looked at each other over Tilda's head.

"Hai! Tego, Timo, wait up," Yanni called, before he and Zander hurried away from Tilda. After a whispered conversation, Tego and Timo—perfect mirror-images of each other—glanced over their shoulders at Tilda. Then all four miners lengthened their strides and caught up with Nico.

Oh, Power. Maybe she shouldn't have said anything. Tilda was too far behind everyone else to hear what was being said, but it was obvious from the waving arms and jabbing fingers that nobody was very happy. She sighed and kept walking.

"Enough!" Nico shouted, whirling round and glaring at his team. "Yes, we'll be working in the old mines to show Lady Matilda where silviron was found. Yes, I am fully aware those mines are more or less stone free and the chances of us finding anything are slim. But we can still dig around a bit to show her how it's done."

"Why in all of Issraya would you agree to this, Nico?" Yanni's face was red, his hands bunched into fists. "If I'd been team leader—"

"Which you're not," Nico bit back. "And perhaps it's about time you let that rest. Feliks chose me, and the sooner you get that into your skull, the better." He glanced round his team. "What else can we do? Do any of you really want to go against Duska, our own powermage?"

Tilda approached cautiously. What would Nico do if they said "yes"? But no one said anything, not even Yanni; there was a lot of foot shuffling and staring at the ground instead.

"Thought not. So let's crack on. The sooner Lady Matilda learns what she needs to, the faster we can get back to normal and go back to where we found the dragon's eye before our mark times out."

"I learn fast," Tilda said, hoping to lighten the mood.

"You'd—"

"—better," the twins snapped.

Chapter 12
Going Underground

EVENTUALLY NICO TURNED off the track onto one that was even narrower. The ground sloped steeply up on either side, and was overgrown up to Tilda's chest in places. She had to push her way through overhanging brambles and huge dock leaves. And it was here that she saw her first mine entrance.

Tilda shivered when she realised what was lying half-hidden under the brambles. The entrance was only a hole, roughly square, cut into the sloping ground. But that hole was deeply black, as though it was sucking all the light around it into its depths. No wonder Duska was terrified of going underground. And she was going to have to step into that herself, if she was going to stand any chance of finding the silviron that the powermages needed to repair the Ringstone.

Tilda shivered again. It simply had to be done, if she wanted to ever draw Power through the Ringstone again.

Nico led the team past several more entrances before he halted. "This is the one we need. We'll be the only ones here."

Tilda stared at the narrow hole, cut here into solid rock. Was that movement in the darkness? Yes—there it was again. The flash of a pale face, the flutter of fabric. She pointed. "We're not. There's someone there."

"What?" Nico twisted round to look. "Dammit!" He dived into the entrance, Yanni close on his heels.

There were cries of alarm, the sounds of a scuffle, and then several figures burst out of the entrance.

"Clear off out of it," Yanni yelled, hauling a man from the tunnel by what was left of the collar on his ragged and patched coat.

The man staggered along the path and fell against Tilda; she shoved him away.

"You've no right," the man yelled in her face. "We got to live somewhere. We ain't doing no 'arm."

Live—here? Tilda recoiled from the beggar's stinking breath and stared, appalled, at the man's stained shirt and fraying trousers. He shoved a fist, encased in blackened and greasy fingerless gloves, into her face.

Tilda backed away.

Nico emerged then, dragging a shrieking bundle of rags with him. "There's a few more, gone deeper in, but I'm not prepared to waste time going after them. At least these two will be out of our way." He let go of the woman and she stumbled, falling onto all fours.

"My fings!" she shrieked.

Nico's answer was to aim a kick at her.

"Nico! Don't," Tilda cried. How could he be so cruel? "She's not doing any harm, let her alone."

The woman looked old—even older than Kamen, and Tilda knew he was *old*. Her dress hung in tatters under a coat which was missing a sleeve. Strips of dirty cloth were wrapped around her hands, and her toes peeped out of the splits in her shoes. A shapeless woollen hat was pulled low over a curtain of lank grey hair. She crawled towards Tilda, sensing an ally.

"They won't 'ave me beggin' in Digdown, miss, and Power knows I've tried. I found others like meself." The woman pointed at the man. "'E tol' me we was alright 'ere cos no one came up this far, to the old mines."

Zander spat on the ground. "Well, he told you wrong. We're here now, so find another entrance to squat in. Get going."

"But my fings," the woman wailed again.

"You've no right," the man repeated. "No right."

Tilda frowned. "Is it really so bad if we let them stay?"

Nico spun towards her. "And when they tell other folk where we're working?" He moved close enough to speak directly into her ear, his voice low. "With a powermage? I thought you wanted to be treated as one of the team, didn't want any special attention, Lady Matilda."

"I do. I don't."

Nico was right, wasn't he? They couldn't afford to advertise what they were doing too widely . . . Tilda had come up with a cover story to explain their presence here to other mining teams if questions were asked, but what if these beggars heard something that cast doubt on the fabrication? What if somehow, Luisa heard about it? True, she'd not been seen on Ring Isle since the battle over the Power and before the problem with the Ringstone was discovered, but she was still out there somewhere. If she heard that a powermage was sniffing round the old mines with a crack team of miners where silviron had once been found . . . She'd be bound to put two and two together, make four hundred. She might try to prevent Tilda from fulfilling her task. Or worse, might risk another attack on Ring Isle if she thought the mages were in a weakened position.

Maybe it *was* better for all of them if the beggars moved on.

"At least let them get their things before you send them away," Tilda muttered.

"Our fings . . . You'll let us get our fings, Lady?"

Power, the beggar *had* heard what Nico said. Tilda went cold.

Nico threw his hands in the air with a snort of disgust. He spun on his heel and headed back into the mine.

"We won't say nuffin about no mage, I promise we won't," the woman gabbled. "I can keep a secret, me. He will, too." She pointed at the other beggar; he sniffed and wiped his nose on the back of his gloved hand, leaving a sticky trail.

Nico came out of the tunnel again and slung a patched bag, a couple of grubby blankets, and a cooking pot on the ground. "Here's your stuff. Now get going."

"Fank you, sir, fank you." The woman snatched up the bag and held it close while the man darted forward to grab the blankets and pot.

Tilda stepped closer to them both. "You really can't tell anyone about me, do you understand?"

For a split second she stared into the man's eyes. Something dark flashed there and Tilda's stomach gave a jolt. Then he looked away, and lolloped away down the track, trailing blankets in the dust. In a strange half-crouch over her bag, the woman scuttled away behind him.

"Now that's sorted, perhaps we can finally go under," Yanni said.

When everyone was standing just inside the mine entrance, Nico addressed the team.

"Normal rules apply." Then he looked straight at Tilda. "No wandering off on your own to explore. You listen to my team, and you listen to me. Do as you're told, understand?"

Tilda nodded. She wasn't about to go exploring in this terrible pressing dark.

"Everyone ready? Let's go."

Walking further into the tunnel didn't seem so bad to begin with. There was light shining in from outside—enough that Tilda could clearly see the rough-hewn walls and the timber props shoring up where the rock gave way to earth. And she could still see Nico walking in front of her. But the further he moved into the tunnel, the more he sank into shadow. The air grew colder and Tilda felt as though the walls were closing in on her. The tunnel ahead bent sharply to the right, but before she reached that point, she felt a tap on her shoulder.

"Take a look behind," Zander said.

Tilda did, and a shiver ran down her spine. A long way behind Zander and the rest of the team was a slash of bright light, all that remained visible of the entrance and the outside world.

"Make the most of it." Zander struck a long match and lit Tilda's helmet lamp before lighting her own. "It's candlelight only from here on in."

She wasn't kidding. As soon as Tilda turned the corner, she saw exactly what Zander meant. Up ahead, Nico was thrown into silhouette as his lamplight bounced off the rocks in front of him. There was nothing but blackness in the space between them. Tilda quickened her pace, determined to keep the blackness and the space to a minimum. What she wouldn't give to be allowed to produce an illuminorb right now. Its light would surely be better—steadier— than that provided by the flickering candles; they sent eerie shadows dancing along the uneven walls.

The ground sloped gently down, taking Tilda deeper into the earth. The walls were no longer dry, but glistening with seeping moisture. There must be tons and tons of rock and soil above her. She imagined the weight of it all crashing down and squashing her flat, then something cold and wet landed on the back of her neck.

She yelped. "I got dripped on!"

"These tunnels aren't that far underground, so water seeps through easily." Nico's voice echoed back to her. "But they are long and there are many branches, like that one." He turned his head slightly, illuminating the opening to another tunnel. "They lead to the oldest of workings, with many too dangerous to go down because of rock falls."

Nico's lamp had shone briefly on something above the opening. As Tilda passed the same place, she trained her own light there and saw a symbol, like a capital "A," with the line across it at an angle, carved into the stone.

"What's that?"

"Miner's mark," Zander told her. "When miners dig tunnels they lay claim to them by marking each of them. Not sure who that one belonged to. Nico might know." She prodded Tilda. "Keep walking."

"So do you have a miner's mark?" Tilda tried to reduce the gap that had opened up again between her and Nico.

"Nah. We have team ones now. You'll see ours if we find anything worthwhile. Though that's unlikely in these old tunnels."

Ahead of them, Nico had stopped. He stuck his head into a narrow gap in the tunnel wall. "We'll try our luck in here," he said as he pulled his head back out. "Stones were found once, cos it's marked, and there's plenty of wall still to go at. It's as good a place as any to show Lady Matilda how we work."

Tilda bristled at the emphasis he placed on her name. "Look, it's silly having to call me Lady Matilda all the time. Just call me Tilda while we're together. Please."

"If that's what you want." Nico disappeared through the gap.

Tilda checked above the entrance. The same miner's mark was scratched into the rock here. Who had the miner with the A symbol been? How long ago had he—or she—worked these tunnels? Maybe they'd never know. She squeezed herself after Nico, and once the rest of the team followed, their combined candlelight illuminated a small cavern. Tilda turned slowly, taking it all in, while everyone else got busy.

Nico inspected the walls, tapping the rock in some places and scraping earth away at others. Zander unpacked several small lanterns and once they were lit, set them on outcrops of stone. The twins unpacked short handled, heavy picks, and Yanni screwed a wooden handle into a short shovel to lengthen it.

Very faintly, Tilda heard music. Just a simple run of perhaps five or six notes, sounding as though they came from a long way off.

"Right. Chipper's going to start there." Nico straightened up and pointed to a place near to the outside edge of a large rock. Then he swept his arm out to the right, over the earth packed hard beside it. "Hackers, clear this next section up to here." He drew a line in the packed earth. "Don't need to tell our Worm what to do, do I?"

Chipper? Hacker? Worm? Tilda looked at Nico, confused.

"I'm Marker. I decide where we're going to dig," he explained. "Zander's the Chipper, cuts into the rock and sees whether I'm right. At least to start with. The twins are Hackers, use their strength to do the hard digging, and our Worm clears the soil away from the working area and piles it up out of the way. For the moment, you'll be another Worm."

"Here you go," Yanni said, thrusting another shovel at Tilda.

It was hard work. Within a couple of hours, Tilda's shoulders ached, her hands were blistered, and there seemed no end to the loose earth and rock chips which needed to be cleared. She felt a welcome relief when Nico called a halt so they could eat.

Tilda sat with the others and dug into her pack. She pulled out the bottle first and drank in greedy gulps to wash the dryness from her throat. Then she unwrapped Gerty's parcel. Inside was a large rectangular pastry, its middle puffed up. One half was marked with lines, the other had a rolled crust. She sniffed it, cautiously.

"Your first miner pie," Zander said. "Just so you know, always start at the lined end."

"Why?"

"Because that end's got meat and tatoes in it," Tego said.

"And the crust end's got fruit," his twin added. "A whole meal in a pastry parcel."

"But don't eat the crust," Nico added. "That's for you to hold, 'cos your hands are mucky."

Everyone fell silent as they tucked in. Tilda had to admit, as pies went, this one was rather good. Chicken and potato one end, apple and bramble jelly at the other. It was a little strange, where meat and fruit combined in the very middle, but she was too hungry to care.

Without the sound of picks and shovels and scraping earth, it was possible to hear smaller sounds; the drip of water, Yanni chewing, and to Tilda's surprise, the music again. She stopped eating and listened carefully. It was the same tune she'd heard before, but louder now. Where was it coming from? After hearing three or four repeats of the notes, Tilda tried whistling it.

"No whistling!" Nico frowned at her. "Bad luck in a mine."

"Sorry."

Tilda might have stopped whistling, but the music carried on without her, repeating itself over and over. It got into her head . . .

Nico finished eating, got up, and pressed his ear close to where they'd been digging.

"What's he doing that for?" Tilda whispered to Yanni.

Yanni shrugged. "Dunno, but he always does. You finished eating? Best get back to work."

Tilda groaned, picked up her shovel, and set to clearing again.

."Got it!" Zander shouted a few minutes later and stepped back quickly.

A large lump of stone fell away from the face where she'd been chipping and landed on the floor with a thump. The music—that same sequence of notes—grew louder still and Tilda looked round in confusion. Where in Power's name was it coming from? Then Nico held a lantern close to the broken rock, and she ignored the music and crowded in with everyone else to see what Zander had found.

"Wouldya look at that." Timo's teeth were very white in the semi darkness as he grinned.

"What are we looking at?" Tilda craned her neck. All she could see was a change in the colour of the rock. It was paler, with a dark green line running through it.

"That, there, is a seam of tomasite, or poor man's emeralt."

"Emeralts?" She peered closer. "Really?"

"Poor man's version of 'em, not the real thing. It don't look much now, but once it's been chipped out, cut, polished . . . There'll be a fair few fancy stones in that lot." Nico ran a hand along the line. "Well done, Zander. This mine's not such a write-off after all. Let's get it out, shall we?" He stepped aside to allow Zander to begin chipping again. Under his breath, he was humming the same music—the same notes—that Tilda had tried to whistle.

Tilda stared at him. "What is that?"

Nico stopped humming and sighed. "I told you, it's tomasite, or poor man's emeralts."

"No, I don't mean that. I'm talking about the music."

Nico's head turned towards her so fast, his neck cracked. "Music?"

"Yes, you know." She hummed the little sequence and then yelped when Nico grabbed her arm and brought his face close to hers.

"You hear nothing," he hissed. "Understand?"

"But I—"

"Nothing!" He pushed her away. "Now, are you going to help the team or just stand watching?"

Tilda rubbed her arm. Why in Power's name wouldn't he admit to hearing the music? And why did she have to pretend she couldn't hear it, either? She glanced at the rock wall, where everyone was now busy chipping away with small hammers and chisels along the length of tomasite. No one else seemed to be able to hear the music, even though it was louder now than at any time before.

"I'll help," she muttered.

When she chipped away a marble sized chunk of the tomasite and held it in her hand, Tilda finally worked out where the music was coming from: the stone. The stone had music, music which she could hear.

Should she say anything? No, everyone would think she was mad—look at how Nico had reacted. Mind you, he'd been humming the same tune. Was it possible that he . . . ? She needed to think about this.

Checking first that Nico was busy loading the chipped stones into a pouch, she nudged Zander. "Can I keep this one? Sort of a momento of my first find," she asked, keeping her voice low.

Zander took the stone and inspected it before handing it back. "Suppose so. Tomasite isn't worth much. That little piece? About two bits, that's all. Won't make much difference to Feliks, or us, if we don't add it to the pouch. We made enough on that dragon's eye to keep us in circoins for a while yet."

"Thank you," Tilda said and slipped the chunk of singing stone into her pocket, muffling its music.

Chapter 13
Dinner at Gerty's

THE TEAM WAS in a good mood when they finally emerged, blinking and shielding their eyes, into late afternoon sun.

"We've found more in there than I thought we would." Zander twirled the end of her plait as they traipsed back down the overgrown track. "Maybe having a mage with us brought us luck."

"Ha! It's our very own Sparkles who finds the stones, not the Power," Yanni snorted. "I swear he sniffs them out."

Perhaps he hears them, Tilda *didn't* say.

"Here, stick these on for a bit," Tego said, offering her a pair of smoked glasses.

"Thanks." She slipped them on, and felt her face unscrunch from a squint.

"Those beggars haven't gone far." Yanni flicked his head towards the trees.

Sure enough, the man and woman were loitering at the edge of them.

"D'you find much, Lady?" the woman called in her cracked voice.

"Clear off, will you?" Nico shouted.

"Leave her," Tilda snapped. "She's doing what you asked and keeping out of your tunnels." But she couldn't help noticing, when she'd passed, that the beggars began to creep back towards the entrance of the mine.

Tilda was exhausted. Her shoulders and arms felt leaden, her legs and back ached, she was caked in a fine layer of earth, and to top it all she was confused. All she could think about was the singing stone—and why Nico wouldn't admit to being able to hear it.

"So who's first in the tub tonight then? Our new Worm?"

Tilda looked up. "What, me?" For a second or two, she imagined the bliss of a hot bath, the warmth easing her aching muscles . . .

"Nope." Nico stared straight ahead. "Tilda's on the rota, same as the rest of you. And you know it's last to join the team, last in on their first day."

"Ooh . . ." Yanni walked backwards along the path, the better to see Tilda's reaction. "No powermage's privilege then?"

She did her best to keep her face from betraying her disappointment, but something must've shown, because Yanni grinned.

"How d'you like that, Worm number two? All five of us in the tub before you. It'll be a bit scummy by the time you get in."

Determined not to react, she shrugged that off. "I wanted to know what it was like to be a miner. If that means being last in the bath, fair enough."

From the corner of her eye, she caught Nico glancing at her. Was he hoping that she would make a scene? Well, she wouldn't give him the satisfaction.

Yanni laughed. "We'll see if you still think it fair when you come out muckier than you went in." He turned round and began to jog.

"Yanni, I'm warning you. No queue jumping," Nico shouted after him.

Zander sped up too. "I'll make sure he doesn't. It's me first tonight."

By the time they reached Main Street, Tilda could barely put one foot in front of the other. If this is what she was like after only one day, how would she ever get up to work another tomorrow?

Nico dropped back to walk beside her. "You alright?"

"Tired."

He nodded. "Takes a while to get used to it."

They walked in silence for a while, Tilda's mind racing. Should she try to ask Nico about the music again? It might make her sound crazy, to be sure, but hadn't she thought she was crazy when she first saw the glow of coloured light at the Ringstone? When she'd felt the tingle of Power in the water of the River Ambak? And when she first heard the voice of her portion of the Power?

Was the music anything to do with the Power? There'd been no tell-tale glow of coloured light, none of the tingling energy she associated with touching it. Only the music—the stonesong, as she was beginning to think of it. The stonesong that she was convinced Nico could hear, in spite of his denial.

Before she could stop herself, she'd opened her mouth. "You can hear music in the stones, can't you?"

"Tosh," Nico said, but he glanced round, checking for—what?

Tilda lowered her voice. "You can. That's how you find the good stones, isn't it? I saw you, leaning against the rock, listening—"

"You're talking rot," Nico hissed. "Shut up!"

"But it might be important, because—"

He rounded on her then. "Do you want to continue with my team? Because if you do, you stop talking about stone songs, got it?"

So he *could* hear it. "Stone *songs*," he'd said. Plural. It wasn't a phenomenon linked only to poor man's emeralts.

Tilda held up her hands in apparent surrender. "Alright, alright. Power knows I like your team, and I don't want to have to move to another one. I won't say anything more about stone songs." She tried to look innocent, but had she pushed Nico too far in mentioning the music again?

"Good. Now hurry up, will you? Otherwise we'll not have time for our baths before it's dinner."

It felt like a long time and an even longer walk before Tilda found herself outside Gerty's turquoise door. Not that she went in through it, of course; Nico opened the plain wooden one.

Gerty looked up from sweeping the bare boards of the "mud" side of the hallway. "Wondered where you'd got to," she said, running sharp eyes over Tilda. "I've been waiting to mop."

"Sorry, Gertie. Tilda didn't walk very fast after her first day."

"Aye, I bet she didn't. Well, there's three of them washed up already, and the fourth's about to come out."

Nico swung his bag off his back. "I hope Zander beat Yanni to the tub."

Gerty chuckled. "She did. So did Timo and Tego. Yanni's just finishing up."

"I'll be in next. Tilda's last."

"Is that so?" Gerty's eyes flicked towards Tilda before casting Nico a shrewd look. "Not long 'til supper—you'd best get scrubbed up."

Nico opened the changing room door and disappeared inside. Tilda would have followed him, but Gerty put a hand on her arm and stopped her.

"I've water heating, ready for washing the floor. I can't make the water any cleaner, but I can warm it up a bit if you'd like, Lady Matilda?"

To Tilda's horror, she felt tears prickling her eyes at this small kindness. "Thanks, Gerty. And please, call me Tilda while I'm under your roof."

Gerty nodded, took her hand from Tilda's arm, and headed along the corridor.

With the door of her box tightly closed, Tilda dropped thankfully onto the bench seat. She fumbled at the laces with tired fingers before she managed to pull off her boots and push them under the seat. She hauled herself to her feet, stripped off her dirty work clothes, and dropped them on the floor.

A buzzer sounded, startling her.

"That's me in the tub," Nico called. His box door banged open. "Next time you hear it, you're in, Tilda."

"Alright."

There was a large, rough towel on the first shelf; Tilda wrapped it round herself and pulled a set of clean clothes from the bag she'd left here—Power—only this morning. All she had to do now was wait for the buzzer.

Suddenly, she remembered the chunk of tomasite and dug into the pocket of her trousers. She pulled it out and turned the chunk of green stone over and over, trying to catch a glimpse of the gem it would become. But she couldn't see it. To her untrained eye, it was only a lump of green stone.

Was it still singing? Tilda held it close to her ear and strained to hear the notes she'd heard in the mine. They *were* there, but very, very faint—a mere whisper compared to what they had been before. The ability to hear the music obviously wasn't a mage thing, otherwise Nico wouldn't be able to hear it, and the skill must be really useful to a miner. How much time would it save, being able to home in on stones because you could hear them?

A little knot of excitement tied itself tight and deep in Tilda's stomach then. If stones had music, might silviron have a song too? And if it did, would that be something she could use to find the fallen starmetal that her portion of Power had said was still to be discovered? Would she be able to hear silviron music in the same way she could hear stone song?

The buzzer sounded. Tilda picked up her clean clothes, stuck the tomasite into the pocket of those trousers, and left her box. She opened the bathroom door cautiously, in case Nico was still there.

He wasn't, but Gerty was; she was dipping a bucket into the tin tub positioned in the middle of the room.

"Thought I'd take some out before I added the hot. Make it go further," she said, swapping the filled bucket for another on the floor beside her; she tipped that one's steaming contents into the tub. "You get in there, quick." She picked up the bucket of dirty water. "You'll feel better when you're scrubbed up."

With the door closed and locked behind Gerty, Tilda set her clothes on a waiting chair. She tiptoed over to the tub and peered into it. Yanni was right; there was a lot of scum. She tried not to mind too much as she dropped the towel and eased herself into the warmish water with a sigh.

Less than a quarter of an hour later, she emerged from the bathroom, pink and tingling after a thorough scrubbing. How strange it was, to enter the house through one door a dirty miner, and be spat out clean and respectable through another.

Tilda followed the voices she could hear down the corridor, which was carpeted here—and therefore "clean"—rather than plain "mud" boards. To the right at the end of the corridor was a steep and narrow staircase; she supposed she'd be climbing that later, when it was time to go to bed. To the left of the stairs was a door; the voices were coming from behind it.

Tilda took a deep breath and pushed the door open.

She walked into a snug kitchen, full of well scrubbed table and miners. Every member of the team was busy, laying places or filling water jugs.

Gerty turned away from the stove with large dish in her hands. "Take your seats, fellas, please! The pie won't keep warm for long."

Tilda joined in the unseemly scramble for seats and ended up sandwiched between the twins.

"Help yourselves to veg," Gerty urged. From her place at the head of the table, she cut huge slices of pie, which eager hands held plates out to receive.

Tilda piled fluffy mashed potato and buttered carrots beside her pie. Following Yanni's lead she picked up her knife and fork, but dropped them again when Yanni yelped.

There was a bright red mark, edged with gravy, across the back of Yanni's hand, and there was a gravied serving spoon in Gerty's hand. Power, the team mother's reactions must be fast; Tilda hadn't even seen her move.

"You know it's Blessing first," Gerty said, scowling at Yanni. "Power of Nargan feed us. Power of Ambak, water us. Power of

Pergatt, enrich us. Power of Merjan, educate us. Power of Kradlock, keep us. Thanks be to the Power."

"Thanks be to the Power," Tilda muttered with the others.

Tego nudged her. "You can eat now."

Tilda picked up her cutlery again and tucked in. Power, but she was hungry.

When everyone's plates were empty after second helpings—and in Tego's case, thirds—Nico was persuaded to show Gerty the tomasite. He shook the stones out onto the table and Tilda could hear numerous faint overlapping versions of the five-note sequence she was familiar with. She slipped her hand into her pocket, where her fingers closed around her own smuggled lump of tomasite. If this particular stonesong was already fading after a few hours of being taken from the earth, might some songs fade even before their stones were dug up? Her stomach swooped. Perhaps the remaining silviron, if it had ever had a song, would be silent now, after millennia underground.

She was going to have to find out more about stonesongs, but it was obvious that she'd have to find the answers herself. Especially if Nico wasn't going to admit to what he could hear and help her.

Gerty finished admiring the poor man's emeralts and dished up cinnamon-scented stewed apples for pudding. "So where'd you find these beauties?"

"The old mines," Zander said, tossing a chunk of tomasite into the air and catching it.

Gerty jumped so violently, she dropped the spoon into the apples.

Tego fished it out of the bowl and licked it clean. "What's up, Gerty?" he said, handing her another spoon.

A flush spread across Gerty's cheeks and her hand trembled as she set Timo's bowl in front of him. "Nothing, just . . . You don't mean Arkanal's mines, do you? You've not been digging there?"

Arkanal. Yes, the miner's mark had looked like a capital A, hadn't it?

Nico nodded. "Tilda wanted to see where silviron was found as well as learn mining. Thought it made sense to go up to Arkanal's and kill two birds with one stone. Plus there weren't going to be too many other teams nosing about and asking awkward questions."

Tilda's heart gave a leap. How close, exactly, had they been to where the silviron had been dug up?

"That's because most of them avoid those tunnels. Wouldn't go in, even if you paid them." Gerty filled another bowl.

"Well, we're being paid. And we'll be back there again tomorrow, see what else we can uncover where we found this lot." Nico swept all the tomasite back into the pouch.

Gerty frowned. "Are you sure you ought to?" Her gaze ran round the table. "I mean, you do know what happened in those old mines, don't you?"

"Course." Yanni sounded confident. "They found silviron there."

"Not just silviron." Gerty shivered. "That's where Arkanal found the black ruby."

The black ruby? Tilda looked up quickly. She'd seen that mentioned in the book Silviu gave her to read. "Isn't the black ruby just a legend?" Everyone turned towards her, and her cheeks grew warm. "I saw it mentioned in a book, don't know anything else about it."

Gerty nodded. "Aye, there's a legend. It's why no one in their right mind goes into those tunnels if they can help it. I'm surprised at you, Nico, thinking of taking a mage down there. I thought Feliks would have stopped you."

Nico spread his hands wide in a helpless gesture. "Maybe Feliks doesn't listen to legends. I certainly don't. And anyway, it's what she"—he jerked his thumb in Tilda's direction—"wanted."

"Will you tell us the legend, Gerty? Please?" Tilda begged. "I'm here to learn, after all. You telling me the story could save me a whole lot of reading, believe me."

A chorus of "go on, Gerty" and "yeah, tell us" followed, until Gerty eventually held her hands up in surrender. "Alright, alright,

I'll tell you. You might think twice about going back tomorrow once you've heard it. Anyone want seconds of pudding before I start?"

With extra helpings dished up to those who wanted them, Gerty placed her hands flat on the table either side of her own empty bowl, as though steadying herself. Then she took a deep breath.

Chapter 14
The Legend of the Black Ruby

"BEFORE THERE WAS ever a Ringstone, there was Power," Gerty began. "It ran deep in the ground of Issraya. And there were many who could draw it from the earth, to effect simple magics of healing and protection."

Something clicked in Tilda's memory. Silviu had mentioned an earthdraw—is that what he'd meant?

"But folk got greedy. Weren't content with simple magics. They drew more and more, used the Power to start hurting, rather than healing. To attack, rather than defend. And it nearly destroyed Issraya."

Tilda nodded. She'd heard a little of this before, from Neesha in Ambak. "But there was a pact. Between the regions."

Gerty nodded. "Aye. It was decided that to stop the misuse, there'd be one place where the Power could be drawn from, and one person from each region allowed to do it on behalf of Issrayans everywhere. Around that time, one of the best for drawing Power here, in Pergatt, was a miner called Arkanal. Everyone thought it'd be him who'd be chosen to be the region's powermage.

"There were others who wanted that role for themselves of course, and they tried to work out what Arkanal's secret was. How did he manage to draw so much Power? But it weren't 'til one bright spark followed him into his mine that they found out." Gerty lowered her voice and looked round her rapt audience. "They saw Arkanal drawing Power through a lump of metal jutting out of the rocks."

"Silviron," Tilda breathed.

"Silviron." Gerty nodded. "Though no one called it that, at first. Course, everyone who fancied themselves as Pergatt's first powermage wanted to draw from the same place, but Arkanal saw how dangerous that would be. Pergattians might be accused of not observing the agreement, and Arkanal could see how other regions might be prepared to fight to get their hands on the metal. So he ordered it to be dug up and sent to Ring Isle, the place chosen as neutral ground where Power could be drawn from by those chosen to be powermages. That way, it'd benefit all the regions equally.

"Folk saw the sense in that notion, so Arkanal and a few other miners set about digging the stuff out. It was them who called it silviron, because it glittered like silver, but was hard as iron. Only problem was, Arkanal didn't just dig up silviron. He found a stone, too."

Yanni snorted. "Not unusual. He was in a mine."

"Ah, but this stone . . ." Gerty actually shivered. "It was black."

"Black?" Nico frowned. "There are no black stones."

"Well, this one was," Gerty said. "Black as shadows, the legend says. Black as a bruise. Black as a world sucked dry of Power."

At that, a shiver ran round the entire table.

Tilda felt sick. She'd seen a blackness like a bruise once before. It had surrounded Luisa in an ugly aura until the Power fought back and sucked it from her, unknowingly contaminating the silviron conduit . . .

"Arkanal lost interest in the silviron, then. Wouldn't let anyone touch his black ruby though, took it everywhere with him. And he carried on doing magics. Unusual, powerful magic. Folk thought he must still be earthdrawing in spite of the agreement, but no one could prove it. What they did see was him holding his black ruby, talking to it in a language no one understood. Folk became afeared of Arkanal, thought he'd gone mad. And then, it happened."

"What?"

Tilda couldn't be sure whether it was one or all of Gerty's audience—herself included—who asked the question, but tension thickened the air as they waited for the answer. She had a horrible suspicion she knew what was coming . . .

"Someone accused Arkanal of continuing to draw. Arkanal denied it, told his accuser the magic came from the black ruby, but he wasn't believed. There was an argument, during which the accuser dropped dead. Folk went after Arkanal of course. He ran, took the black ruby with him. Folk followed, tried to stop him, but he screamed at them not to come close, the stone had made him kill once already and it'd make him kill them, too."

Yanni laughed. "The only way a stone's going to kill you is if it lands on your head."

Gerty shook her head. "Stones have properties, Yanni. You know that. Why else do you have a chunk of rosario hanging round your neck, if not to help you sleep well?"

Yanni's hand strayed to his chest and he blushed.

"Why do the gemsmen make so much of using some stones for love, some for courage, others for patience?" Gerty continued. "Why shouldn't there be a stone capable of killing?"

Power, what a terrible thought. And yet . . . was it the stone itself that had the ability to kill—or the magic contained within it? Tilda had seen the powermages use items they had added Power to. It might be perfectly possible to do the same thing with bad magic, too.

It seemed there was even more to the legend; Tilda forced herself to listen to the rest.

"A mob followed Arkanal to his mine and went in after him. But he never came out." Gerty shook her head.

"He got lost in the tunnels?" Nico banged his hand on the table. "Haven't I always said you need to be careful, however well you think you know them?"

"Oh, it was worse than that. Only one or two of those who'd followed Arkanal into the mine ever came out again. They told what happened." Gerty swallowed hard. "They found Arkanal at last, near to where the silviron had been taken from. He was clutching the ruby, screaming something about how he wouldn't let it hurt anyone else. They said his shadow grew huge around him, black as midnight. Then the tunnel exploded and buried him, and most of those who'd chased him, under tons of rock and earth."

Shock rippled around the table; Tilda felt as though she'd been kicked in the gut.

"The legend says that somewhere in Arkanal's mine, he lies there still, clutching the black ruby. It's a cursed stone, that one, and best it lays where Arkanal fell, for there's no telling what a man might do if something that terrible was ever found again." Gerty pushed her chair away from the table. "So now you know why you should keep out of Arkanal's mines."

"But . . . how? How could a stone do that?" Zander was frowning, as though she was really trying hard to work it out.

Gerty shrugged and collected the dirty dishes. "Maybe it was another part of the falling star that became our silviron? Maybe it drew a magic or power no one knew existed." She picked up the stack of bowls. "But you mark my words. Don't go looking for that black ruby. Those who've gone searching for it only ever ended up with terrible bad luck. Or dead."

Chapter 15
Sunstone

"BREAKFAST IN FIVE minutes, Worm two," Yanni called through the attic bedroom door the following morning. "Best get a wriggle on."

It felt far too early to be getting up—it was barely light—but Tilda pulled on her clothes, groaning as the muscles in her arms protested after the exertion of the previous day. She entered the kitchen just as Gerty set a plate of ham and eggs down at the only empty place left at the table.

"There you are. Thought you'd overslept." Gerty raised her voice above the noise of conversation and cutlery. "Get that down you. Tea or coffee?"

"Tea, please." Suddenly hungry, Tilda sat down and tucked in. For a few moments, all her focus was on the food, but then she became aware of a heated conversation between Yanni and Nico.

"But imagine finding it," Yanni was saying. "How much would Feliks pay for it, d'you think?"

"I don't know, and I don't care," Nico snapped. "We're not going further into the old mine than we've already been. We found tomasite yesterday, and where there's tomasite, there's usually jennisine. That's what we'll be looking for today. Not some mythical black ruby."

A hush fell over the table; obviously Tilda wasn't the only one listening to the argument.

Yanni persisted. "What if it's real, though? In case you hadn't noticed, there's others in this team, Nico. And we're just as capable of making decisions as you. If we all decide to look for it, you can't—"

"Enough, Yanni. When your decisions start finding us white velvets, I might start listening. Until then, I've told you what we're going to do today. If you don't like my orders, find another team to work with."

Two bright spots of colour burned in Yanni's cheeks. He got up so fast, his chair scraped loudly on the floor. Before anyone could say anything, he was out of the kitchen. The door slammed behind him.

Tilda quickly swallowed the mouthful she'd been chewing. She wasn't exactly keen on digging up a cursed ruby, but if Nico was saying that he wasn't prepared to go deeper into the mine . . . "Does that mean I'm not going to see where the silviron was found then?"

Nico stopped scowling at the door and scowled at Tilda instead. "If you mean the exact place, then you were never going to see that anyway. It was all so long ago, no one remembers *exactly* where it was, only that it was in the old mines somewhere."

"In *Arkanal's* mine," Gerty corrected him.

Tego crossed his arms and stared at Tilda. "Why are you so keen to see the actual place? It's not like you're going to find any more, is it?"

Oh, that was too close to the truth to be comfortable. Yanni was already causing problems with all this talk of the black ruby. Nico wouldn't thank her for telling the team about the very real possibility of finding silviron.

"It just feels important to know." Tilda shrugged. "Call it a powermage's intuition."

"Well, I doubt even your powermage's intuition could find the right tunnel and exact place after so many years." Nico picked up his mug and downed the dregs of his coffee. "We leave in ten minutes. Make sure you're all ready."

Tilda spent the long walk to the mine deep in thought. If no one could remember exactly where the silviron had been dug up in Arkanal's mines, what chance did she have of ever finding the place? There must be miles of tunnels in the oldest section alone. It would be like looking for a grain of sand in a salt pan. A hundred teams of miners working all hours might not be enough to discover silviron—and this was only one team of miners, and she was only one, untrained, powermage. How else could she try to home in on the metal, without alerting Nico and the others?

She knew that silviron was a conduit for the Power. And she knew what Power felt like. At least, she knew what the Merjanian and Ambakian portions of it felt like; the first filled her with fizzing energy, the latter with warmth and comfort. Heck, she could even see the Power—the coloured auras were hard to miss, once you knew what you were looking for. Surely she'd be able to detect the Pergattian portion if it was present? See a green glow, feel . . . something? The Ambakian portion had drawn her to itself, giving her a gentle tug in the right direction when she was looking for the ring. If the Power here was capable of doing the same, and if it concentrated itself near to silviron, well, she might not have to search too hard.

Tilda almost stopped walking. She chewed at her lip, thinking furiously. Maybe she didn't need to use the Power at all. Perhaps she could rely on stones. The tomasite had a song, and she had heard it. Today, they were mining for jennisine, which Nico had said was often found close to tomasite. Did jennisine have a song of its own, too? If it did, if different stones were sometimes found together and each had their own music, then . . . The black ruby had been found with silviron originally, and Arkanal had been close to the original site when the explosion had happened . . . If the *ruby* had a song that she could hear . . . maybe it would lead her to the silviron, regardless of whether the metal had a song or not.

Tilda shook her head. There were far too many *ifs* in that train of thought for comfort, and yet here came another, close behind; if there was *any* kind of singing stone close to what was left of the silviron, would it help?

"Nico," she called, hurrying to catch up with him. "Gerty said the black ruby was found with the silviron, but do you know if there were any other stones found with it?"

"Dunno. Never heard tell of any." Nico shot her a sideways glance. "Why?"

"I just thought that . . ." She musn't appear too eager. "If there were other stones found at the same time as the silviron, and we mined any of them, we'd know we might be close to where the silviron originally came from."

"Huh." Nico nodded. "I can see how that'd work, but the only stone Gerty talked about was the ruby. It doesn't matter if we never find the actual place, though. It'll be a cavern, no different to the one you were in yesterday and which you're going back to today. Isn't that a close enough experience?"

No, Tilda wanted to yell. I *have* to find the right place, find what's left of the silviron, or there'll be no more Power. Ever! But she didn't. Instead, she said, "I suppose so" and followed Nico into the mine without saying another word on the subject.

It was easier this time to step into the darkness, because she knew what to expect. And today, there was no sign of the beggars either inside or outside of the tunnels, which she was grateful for. She didn't relish the thought of another meeting with the angry man.

When the team reached the cavern which had yielded the seam of poor man's emeralts the previous day, as much as Tilda strained to hear it, nothing of the simple stonesong was audible today. They must've dug out every last little piece of tomasite.

"We're looking for jennisine today." Nico scratched a cross on the rock, about a handswidth below where they'd previously dug. "Start chipping here, Zander, while the twins clear the next section again. You know you'll have to go deeper?"

Zander paused in the choosing of a chisel. "Course I do, Sparkles. Sunstone's light don't shine easily, in spite of its name."

How could a stone be named for the sun if it didn't shine?

"Are sunstones another poor man's stone?" Tilda asked, screwing the handle into her shovel.

"I suppose you could say that. They're a fancy stone—" Timo said.

"—but not rare, so they're not expensive." Tego exchanged a grin with his twin. "Popular with young ladies, sunstone. Ain't it, Zander?"

Zander's jaw tightened, and she gave her chisel a hefty whack with the hammer. "Not with me, it's not."

Tilda looked up when the twins sniggered. "Why? Don't you like the colour or something?"

"Nowt to do with colour," Yanni said, speaking for the first time since breakfast. "Sunstone's supposed to increase your feminine charm, and Zander here, as one of the few lady miners in Digdown, ain't exactly at home wearing posh frocks or batting her eyelashes."

"Nope." Zander flourished her tools and grinned. "Give me these and a rock face, and I'm happy. I won't say no to decent stones if we find 'em, but only if I can trade them for cash. I've enough charm already, thanks very much!"

The others howled with laughter.

"We won't find anything at all if you lot don't stop messing," Nico said. "Crack on, can't you?"

For several hours, all Tilda heard was the sound of chipping and hacking and scraping as Zander and the twins worked at the rock and soil until they'd created a hole so wide and deep, Zander could pretty much lie inside it and touch the back wall.

Then Tilda heard music. She paused in her clearing of the debris to listen; this tune was light in feel, had higher notes, almost like a burst of birdsong. She certainly couldn't hum this one—it was far too long and complicated to remember. It meant there were stones, somewhere close. Sunstones? Or something else?

"I reckon we're close," Nico said. "I've got a good feeling about this."

Did he really have a feeling—or could he hear the song? Tilda cleared away the stone chips and earth as fast as she could, eager to see the stone which had such a pretty song.

A few minutes passed before she heard a muffled cheer.

"We've got it," Zander shouted, and passed large chunks of stone out to the others.

Tilda took one and carried it closer to the lantern. It was a dull gold in colour and glittered as the lamplight caught it. A pretty song for a pretty stone, then.

"Colour's not too bad," Nico said, examining another piece. "Would've been better had it been brighter."

Zander backed out of the deep hole. "You might be in luck. Look at this." She handed him another lump, and the team crowded round to see.

Tilda leaned in too and caught her breath. This piece of sunstone was bright yellow, like liquid sunshine. And it sang . . . oh, how it sang!

"Nice," Tego said.

"That'll go for a fair bit more, won't it?" Timo's excitement shone from his face.

"I reckon," Nico said. "If it's brighter the deeper we go, then—"

Something was tickling Tilda's neck. Stray hair? She tried to brush it off, but the tickling sensation remained. It grew stronger, spreading like a vine across her shoulders and down her arms. As it crept towards her chest, there was a sudden jolt of fizzing.

Something had connected with her residual Power.

Tilda's heart thumped against her ribs, the fizzing almost painful in her finger ends. She half-expected to see a tell-tale green glow, but the cavern was still only lit by flickering candle lanterns. She took a step closer to the hole and felt a second jolt; she pressed her hand to her chest. She stepped closer again; this time the tickling sensation grew stronger, the music of the sunstones louder. Except . . .

Every now and again, in the music . . . An odd note or two which didn't seem to fit . . . A bit like when—

"What's up, Tilda?"

She looked up, startled, at Zander. "I don't know. Something doesn't feel . . . right." Those odd notes she could hear. Could it be the song of a different stone? It didn't sound like exactly like a tune, but perhaps . . . "There's something else down there, in the hole."

"You what?" Zander took the candle off her helmet and reached far into the hole. Tilda peered inside, as the rest of the team pressed in around her.

Deep within the diggings the yellow sunstone glittered, and below it, still trapped in the earth, something long and thin glowed white.

Zander's whisper was deafeningly loud in the silence. "Is that—?"

"Bone?" Tego choked.

A sharp crack sounded above Tilda's head. She looked up.

A fine trickle of earth was falling from a gap between two large rocks.

Was that gap getting wider?

One of the rocks shifted. Lumps of earth and small stones pattered onto Tilda's upturned face, there was a loud rumble and—

"Look out!"

A mighty shove sent her stumbling across the cavern, where she fell heavily against a wall. Everything went black, and the music—both the sunstone's song and the odd notes—was smothered by the deafening sound of rocks falling.

Chapter 16
Rockfall

ABSOLUTE, UTTER BLACKNESS.

Had she gone blind? Her eyes were wide open, straining to see the hand she was waving in front of her face, but—nothing.

Panic boiled up inside Tilda and a scream strangled itself in her throat. She was dead. Had to be. Except here was her hand, touching her face—how could she feel that if she was dead? And she wouldn't be able to hear an echoing rumble or the sound of people coughing, either.

The others!

"Nico?" she croaked. "Zander?"

The grittiness in her throat set her coughing until she could barely breathe. Beneath the tightness in her chest, she became aware of another sensation—one she'd almost forgotten about in her panic: fizzing Power. Without thinking, she thrust her hand into the blackness.

"Illuminarka spherus."

An illuminorb sprang to life in her palm, so starkly white against the darkness, it blinded her and left bright spots in her vision. But in that first flash of light, she'd seen them . . .

Timo, cowering against the far wall of the cavern.

Yanni, uncurling from the ground, loose soil falling away as he moved.

Nico, on his hands and knees beside Tilda, the whites of his eyes shining brightly against skin darkened with soil.

And Tego . . .

Timo threw himself onto the crumpled form lying at his feet, with a cry of alarm.

Tego groaned and raised a filthy hand to his head.

"Oh, thank Power, I thought you were done for," Timo gasped.

"I'm not that easy to get rid of." Tego managed a lopsided smile.

The orb light flickered as Tilda lost concentration for a moment; there was a lot of blood running down Tego's face.

"Zander!" Nico shouted, looking wildly around the cavern. "Zan!"

"There!" Yanni pointed at a boot sticking out of a pile of rocks and soil.

"Don't let that light go out," Nico ordered hoarsely, scrambling over the debris towards the boot. With Yanni's help, he flung rocks aside and scooped soil away with his bare hands, racing to uncover their Chipper.

Tilda gritted her teeth and tried to focus on the orb. Would her residual Power last as long as Nico and Yanni needed it to? Or would she plunge them all into the darkness again at any moment? Power forbid it exploded . . .

"Never thought I'd say this," a dazed Zander said as Nico pulled away the last of the dirt and helped her to stand, "but I think sunstone might be my new favourite gem."

"You're not hurt?" Yanni said, in disbelief.

"Bit bruised, but I'll live, thank Power. I dived into the hole, so only my legs got caught." She glanced over at Tilda. "Nice light, Worm."

Tilda grimaced. "Never held one this long. Not sure how much longer . . . I can."

"Find the bags, get candles," Nico ordered. "Just in case."

Was it her imagination, or could Tilda see the illuminorb losing some of its brightness already? She willed every atom of fizzing Power from her body into that little ball of light, holding it steady, keeping them all safe, until finally a hand fell on her shoulder.

"You can let it go," Nico told her. "We've lit the candles."

Thank Power. The illuminorb's white light winked out, leaving a murkier yellow glow in its place. Tilda slumped against a rock, her whole body a mass of aches. It was the longest she'd ever maintained an orb—she ought to be exhausted.

But she wasn't. Power still fizzed inside her. If anything, it felt stronger than before. It was almost as though she'd produced the orb without using any Power at all . . . or as if she'd managed to draw Power as quickly as she'd used it. There'd been that tickling sensation and the jolt of energy, just before the roof collapsed. Did that mean there was Power here somewhere, that she'd drawn on without realising?

An ominous cracking and creaking above her head made her look up. Was more of the roof about to give way?

"Don't worry. The stones do that sometimes after a fall," Nico reassured her.

"The roof collapsed!" Tilda's voice sounded shrill, even to her own ears. "How do we know what's left up there is safe?"

"Look up. See those two huge rocks up there? They won't shift."

She looked and saw, but didn't believe him. He couldn't know for certain that they wouldn't come crashing down as well.

"It happens," Nico continued. "A bit of soil and a few stones give way. It's a pain when it happens, but doesn't normally kill anyone."

"Nico?" Yanni jerked his head towards where Tego was struggling to his feet with the aid of his twin. "Tego doesn't look too good. We need to get him back."

"Right." Nico's tone became businesslike. "Can you and Tilda bring as many of our bags between you as you can carry? I'll give you a hand, Zander. That leg's worse than you're admitting. Timo, can you manage Tego on your own? Good. Let's go."

They moved as fast as Zander's limp and Tego's disorientated stumbles would allow, but it still seemed an age before a bright coin of light appeared ahead of Tilda.

She'd never been so glad to see daylight in her life, when she emerged—last—into the light, struggling under the weight of two bags. Everyone else had stopped a little way beyond the mine entrance; Zander massaged her injured leg while Nico tried to catch his breath from taking her weight, Timo was inspecting his twin's head injury, and Yanni was blowing out the candles.

From behind the trees, beggars appeared. Tilda recognised the man and woman who'd been thrown out of the tunnels, but there were several other men with them now. All just as dirty, just as ragged, and just as curious as they crept towards the team members.

"We heard the fall," said one who Tilda hadn't seen before.

"Got what you deserved by the look of it, after you kicked us out." That was the raggedy man of yesterday. Was he their leader?

"Lady, what happened?" The old woman was the only one who sounded concerned.

"Rockfall," Tilda mumbled. One of the bags started to slip.

The woman rushed forward to try to catch it, but missed. She yelped in pain when a buckle on one of the straps caught on the rags she'd got bound around her right hand, dragging them loose.

Tilda caught a glimpse of a curved, weeping sore on the old woman's palm. "You're hurt? Let me see."

The beggar pulled her hand tight to her chest and shook her head. "Burns from a pan, tis all. Taking a while to heal." She bound the loose rag more securely, re-covering the wound.

Yanni was almost hopping with excitement. "Did you see it, Nico? The bone?"

"Bone?" The leader of the beggars stepped forward, suddenly interested.

Nico ignored him and straightened up. "We don't know that's what it was."

"It was!" Yanni threw his arm out towards the rest of the team. "We all saw it. A long bone, had to be an arm or leg. Could it be—"

Nico gave a hoarse laugh. "What? Arkanal?" He shook his head and dust flew out of his hair. "Gerty's legend's gone to your head, Yanni."

Zander nodded. "Probably just some poor sod who was digging there before us. Or a beggar like one of these, ventured in too far, but wasn't as lucky as we were when the roof came down."

Yanni's eyes were bright. "But it fits the legend, don't it? What if it is Arkanal? And the black ruby's with him?"

"Arkanal's black ruby."

Tilda heard the whisper, but she couldn't be sure which beggar had spoken.

"For Power's sake, Yanni," Nico snapped. "The chances of it being Arkanal is about the same as Zander here wearing a frock down the mine. Just leave it, y'hear? Leave it. We need to get back to town."

Tilda bent to pick up her fallen bag, but the old woman reached it first.

"Let me help."

"Are you sure? What about your hand?"

"Be fine." As though to prove it, the beggar swung the bag onto her shoulder with only the merest hint of a wince.

"You help them? After what they did? Pah!" The leader spat at the woman's feet.

"They let me get my fings," the woman replied, with a shrug. "Kindness for kindness."

It was not a pleasant journey back into town. Yanni wouldn't stop muttering under his breath about bones and black rubies. Zander was managing the pace with Nico's support, but Tego kept slowing them down. It was obvious to all of them from his slurred speech and stumbling feet that he needed help. Fast.

When the first houses came into view, Tilda breathed a sigh of relief. "Almost there." She glanced at the beggar who'd walked beside her all the way.

"Won't go to town. Not welcome," the beggar said, shrugging the bag off her shoulder and laying it at Tilda's feet. "Samya go back."

"Samya. That's your name?"

The woman nodded once, then turned and headed back up the track.

"Thank you, Samya," Tilda called after her.

"Great. We could have done without that. Need all the help we can get, especially over there." Yanni jerked his head towards where Timo sagged under the weight of his injured brother. Tego had turned a ghastly shade of grey under the dust and dirt coating his skin.

Tilda had an idea—something she'd seen sailors do to get older passengers across the gangplanks back home. "Why don't we make a chair?"

"Fetch a chair?" Nico shook his head. "We haven't got time for that."

"No, make one. Clasp your hands with someone else. Like this." Tilda demonstrated. "You can carry him then."

"We could . . ." Nico's eyes narrowed. "If I do that with Timo, then Yanni's going to have to help Zander."

"And what about these?" Yanni indicated the bags he was carrying. "Tilda can't manage any more'n one from here on."

As much as she'd have liked to prove him wrong, Tilda knew Yanni was right. Even the one bag she'd carried down the track felt now as if it was packed with lead.

Nico shrugged. "We'll have to leave most of the bags here then."

"Our tools—" Zander began.

"They'll be nicked!" Yanni finished for her.

"Stick them under a tree and cover them well," Nico said, already linking hands with Timo. "If Tilda can only carry one bag, best she brings the sunstone. At least that way, if our tools *are* stolen, we've the means to pay for new ones."

As the rest of the team organised themselves, Tilda stuffed as much sunstone into one bag as she could carry. By the time she'd pushed all the other bags under a thick clump of brambles and tugged some of the longest briar branches down to hide them, everyone else had already set off and were already a good way down the track.

She hauled the bag of stones onto her back, and it bumped against her spine with every step she ran to catch the others up.

Chapter 17
First Aid

GERTY WAS SHOUTING even as she flung open the turquoise-painted door. "You better have a Power full good reason for pounding so hard on my—" Her eyes widened, taking in the dishevelled team standing on her doorstep.

"Rockfall. Tego's bad," Nico gasped. "Zander's hurt too."

"In, quickly." Gerty's tone was brisk.

Tilda hung back. "But the dirt—"

"Carpets'll clean," Gerty told her. "In, now."

Tilda still tried to knock the worst of the muck off her boots before she stepped inside. She followed everyone else into a small parlour room, which contained several overstuffed chairs and a long couch. Zander sank gratefully into one of the chairs and stretched her leg out, while Nico and Timo settled Tego onto the couch.

Tilda shrugged the bag off her back and set it down in a corner. Sunstone might well be pretty, but Power, it was heavy.

"Where's Yanni?" Gerty said. "He's not—?"

"He's fine." Nico straightened up and rolled his shoulders. "I sent him to fetch Feliks."

"I still think he should've gone for a Medician." Timo sank to his knees beside the couch, fear etched on his face as he stared at his brother. "Will he be alright?"

"Perhaps, if it's only a cut and a touch of concussion," Gerty said, inspecting Tego's wound. "We'll send for a Medician if he gets any worse." She looked up from her inspection and scowled at Nico. "I told you, I did. Nothing good comes of being in Arkanal's mine.

Look at the state of you all! It's thanks to the Power you all made it back."

Nico scowled back. "Rockfalls happen in all mines, Gerty. It was bad luck, that's all, and—"

The front door banged open. "Nico? Gerty?" someone shouted.

Before anyone could shout back, Feliks burst through the parlour door, closely followed by Yanni. And behind him, pausing in the doorway—

"Duska!" Tilda had never been so pleased to see anyone in her life.

"Power protect us," Feliks said, hurrying straight to the couch. "Is he badly hurt?"

Tego stirred and whispered, "Be back an' digg'n 'fore y'can say . . . sunstone."

"No, you won't. Not if I have anything to do with it." Feliks ran a pale hand through his hair. "You're all on a break until I say differently."

"But what about the ruby?" Yanni blurted out.

Feliks spun towards him. "What ruby?"

"Don't listen to him," Nico snapped. "We found tomasite and jennisine, but he's still banging on about something that doesn't exist."

"We all saw the bone," Yanni shot back. "If that's Arkanal, we need to—"

"You can't be serious—"

"Did you get a bang on the bonce, too?"

"Who's the team leader here?"

Everybody started talking at once.

Tilda flinched at the noise. Across the room, she caught Duska's eye; the mage inclined her head towards the door and stepped into the corridor. A quick glance around the room was enough to convince Tilda that everyone else was too busy trying to be heard to notice whether she was there or not. She slipped quietly into the corridor too.

Duska took Tilda into the kitchen. She pushed the door almost closed, muting the sound of arguments in the parlour. "Are you alright, Tilda?"

"I think so."

Except maybe she wasn't. Somehow, the safety and normality of Gerty's kitchen made Tilda's near miss seem like a nightmare. What if . . . ? Her knees buckled and she almost fell into a chair. Why wouldn't her hands stop shaking?

"Hmmm." Duska pointed at Tilda's face. "You've got a good bruise coming there."

"Have I?" Tilda touched her cheekbone and winced. It was rather tender. "I didn't realise."

Duska leaned on the table. "We don't have much time to talk. What did you find? Other than this mythical ruby that Yanni's talking about."

Tilda shook her head. "Nothing. But I think he's right. There is . . . something down there."

Duska's eyes narrowed. "What sort of something?"

"I don't know, but there's music." Tilda clasped her hands together to stop them shaking. "A song. The gemstones sing."

"Yes." Duska nodded. "They do. I hear them sometimes."

"Really?" Tilda sat up straighter. "Is it only supposed to be powermages that hear it?"

"No. It's a talent that appears every now and again in a Pergattian. Some miners have been known to . . . oh." Duska smiled. "That's why Feliks' team is so good, isn't it? One of them can hear stonesong?"

"Nico," Tilda admitted. "But he won't talk about it."

"Hmm." Duska leaned back. "Probably for the best. It causes problems when other miners find out. They think it gives a team an unfair advantage when it comes to mining."

Tilda frowned. "Why can I hear it then? I'm Merjanian, not Pergattian."

"True." Duska fell silent. "Your father was Pergattian, though, wasn't he?"

"Yes."

That might explain it. Just like she'd inherited Pa's eyes, maybe something else deep inside Tilda was linked more closely to his home region than she'd ever realised.

"Duska, I wondered if . . . well, does silviron sing?"

"Not that I'm aware of. Why?"

Tilda chewed her lip. So that other strange music she'd heard, immediately before the rockfall, couldn't have been silviron. Dammit. Even though she'd felt that jolt of Power, the tickling . . . "There was a feeling, I thought perhaps it was Power. It tickled."

"The Pergattian portion does not tickle." Duska actually looked offended. "It is strong, vibrant. It dances."

"Oh." It danced? Tilda had no idea what that must feel like, but if the tickling she'd experienced wasn't Pergattian Power, it didn't explain why she had managed to hold the orb for so long without her own Power being depleted. Would Duska be angry with her for making the orb, even in an emergency? She'd better find out. "I . . . made an orb. After the roof collapsed. And my Power didn't run out, so I thought, perhaps—"

"You're improving, that's all. Focusing the Power better in how you use it, rather than wasting it." Duska sighed and straightened up. "You made the right decision to produce an orb, but you must take care not to use more Power than is absolutely necessary. If you drain yourself completely . . ."

Tilda was all too aware of the consequences. Sitting this close to Duska, she could see the mage's face was pale, her eyes darkened by shadows. Was Duska already beginning to feel the effects of a lack of Power? An image flashed into Tilda's head; Silviu, unrecognisably aged when she'd returned to Ring Isle after finding the ring. If that was to be the fate of them all if they couldn't find silviron . . . She shivered.

Duska was shaking her head. "I'm not sure you ought to go back into the mine, Tilda. Silviu won't thank me if anything happens to you. I need to rethink how we search for the silviron. Perhaps make it public knowledge, get more teams involved."

"But won't it scare people if they know what we're looking for? They'll want to know why." Her one chance to be of real use, and the rockfall was going to snatch it away from her. She wasn't ready to give up so easily. There was something singing in Arkanal's mine, and there was Power; she wanted to find both. It might even lead her to silviron . . . She *had* to carry on. "Can't I go back with Nico's team for a few more days before you involve anyone else?"

Duska shook her head. "I'm sorry, Tilda. It's proving far too dangerous. Perhaps we should have been more open from the start."

"But—"

"The most I will grant you," Duska continued, "is that you may go down with Feliks' team once more, when they have had the rest that their Master has imposed. Then we will find others to help in our search."

The door opened then, and Feliks walked in. "Ah, here you are. The good news is that Tego seems to be perking up somewhat." He rubbed his forehead. "He had me worried for a moment or two. That rockfall was worth it though. Quite a haul of sunstone. Nico's going to come with me and bring the stones so I can put them in the safe at the office. I hate to ask, Tilda, but would you go with Yanni, bring back the bags? I don't fancy leaving them hidden any longer than they need to be."

All she wanted was a bath, something to eat, and her bed, but Tilda knew she couldn't let Nico and the rest of the team down. She'd wanted to muck in with them—it would be unfair for her to claim any privileges for being a powermage after what they'd all experienced. She glanced down at the briar scratches on her hand. There'd be a few more of those when she came back with the bags.

"Of course." She stood up. "We'll be back for supper."

Chapter 18
Bones

THE BAGS WERE still there when Tilda and Yanni reached the place where she'd left them. She hauled them out one by one, gritting her teeth as the brambles snagged on her hands and arms.

Yanni emptied the tools out and checked them over. "Nothing missing, thank Power. As soon as Feliks gives the word, we'll be back to digging." Then he looked up at Tilda. "D'you think there really is a black ruby?"

"I don't know." Tilda squatted beside him. She'd heard something, certainly. The most likely explanation for the music was that there was another stone waiting to see daylight. Whether it was the black ruby of legend or something else entirely, she couldn't tell by sound alone. She'd never find out either, until she was allowed back into the mine.

She watched as Yanni began to repack the bags. There had definitely been Power in the cavern too—she'd felt it! But was it linked to the presence of starmetal? Perhaps.

She'd never be able to prove it though, because the rockfall had forced her out of the mine. She needed to go back to the cavern *now* to answer these questions, not in a few days time when the rest of the team were fit and well. And definitely before Duska started to involve more teams of miners, who'd be all over these tunnels like a rash.

Her opportunity to solve the mysteries or carry on searching was slipping away, all because she had to wait.

The idea hit her then so forcefully, she gasped and fell back onto her bottom. There, on the grass in front of her, were all the tools a miner needed. She *could* do her own digging. Right now. Not when Feliks said she could, or when Duska had found extra help.

Tilda pulled one of the empty bags towards her, snatched up a chisel and hammer, and shoved them inside it.

"Er . . . what are you doing?"

What else would she need? Candles, a short shovel and handle, a pick.

"I'm going back down."

"Into the mine?" Yanni grabbed her arm. "But you can't. Feliks said—"

Tilda shook him off and yanked the bag shut. "I don't answer to Feliks. I'm a powermage and I am going back because I think we missed something. You can go back, tell him if you like. I don't care." She scrambled to her feet. "Who knows, I might even find that black ruby."

"Are you serious?" Yanni's eyes widened.

"I'm serious." She turned away and walked along the path, her insides quivering. She was an idiot even to consider going into the mine on her own. She'd only mentioned the ruby because she hoped—Power, please!—that Yanni would take the bait and go back under with her.

"Who made you an expert on stones all of a sudden?" Yanni called.

"No one." She kept walking. A few moments later, she heard footsteps behind her and glanced over her shoulder.

Yanni didn't look happy, but he'd caught her up, and he had bag slung over his shoulder too. "What'll happen when the Lady Duska finds out her little powermage isn't obeying instructions?"

What indeed? Tilda hoped her face didn't show any of the uncertainty she was feeling. "Let's hope she doesn't. At least, not until we have something to tell her."

"If we find that ruby, we split the sale, fifty-fifty." Yanni spat on his palm and held his hand out.

Tilda barely hesitated. She spat into her own palm and shook Yanni's hand. "Fifty-fifty." Afterwards, she wiped her hand down her trousers.

Tired as they both were, they made good time back to the mine. The little band of beggars were there of course, huddled around a campfire at the edge of the trees. Only Samya looked up; Tilda felt the woman's eyes on her, but the beggar didn't say a word, and she was glad of it. The last thing she needed right now was any of the beggars poking their noses in.

The sound of footsteps echoed along the tunnels, bouncing back and forth until it sounded as though there were an army of miners tramping towards the cavern, not just two.

A shiver ran down Tilda's spine when she reached the cavern she'd so recently left. The floor was covered in fresh earth and large stones, some of it trodden down or pushed aside by the team's rescue efforts. She picked her way across the cavern to where Zander and the sunstone had been dug out. She peered in.

"I can't see anything that looks like bone now. There's too much debris inside. I'll have to clear that out of the way first." She glanced over her shoulder at Yanni. "Ready, Worm?"

He scowled and pulled the shovel from his bag.

Tilda wanted—no, she needed—to dig. She'd take the full blame for disobeying orders herself, tell Duska and Feliks that Yanni hadn't wanted to help but that she'd forced him to. There was something in this cavern, close to this hole, that she didn't understand. She had to find out what it was.

She could still hear a trace of sunstone music, and the more soil she cleared from the hole, the louder and clearer it became. And the louder and clearer it became, the more she could pick out the other music, those peculiar notes that didn't seem to fit.

She dragged another shovelful of soil behind her and saw the flash of white. "Found it!"

"What? What have you found?"

The light inside the hole dimmed as Yanni blocked the entrance to it and peered in.

"Hang on." Tilda cleared the soil away carefully with her hands, trying not to move the fragments of ivory as she uncovered them. It *was* bone. The fragments lay close to a large rock; Tilda worked outwards from there, uncovering longer and more intact pieces. Were they part of a leg, or an arm? At the far end of them were smaller unbroken pieces, laid roughly in lines . . . Could they be . . . . fingers? Her stomach gave an uncomfortable lurch. Someone had died here, a long time ago, when this enormous boulder had fallen on them.

She slid her shovel underneath one of the larger fragments and lifted it up, along with the earth it sat on. Then she backed out of the hole.

"Let's have a look," Yanni said. He picked up the fragment and inspected it closely. "Oh, that's definitely bone. Is there any more in there?"

Tilda nodded. "Yes. I think . . ." She swallowed hard. "I think it's an arm. It's been there a long time. The rest of the skeleton's underneath a massive rock which stopped me digging any further." Her stomach jolted again, imagining the poor miner's final moments.

"Arkanal." Yanni stared at the bone he was holding. "It has to be. But we'll only know for sure if we find the black ruby as well."

There was a sound, beyond the cavern. The skittering of small stones across rock. Tilda's heart missed a beat. Not another rockfall? But as the echoes faded, sounding more like footsteps than a tunnel collapse, she breathed more easily. In the silence, she could hear that odd little phrase of music quite clearly, coming from the hole.

And from the sliver of bone in Yanni's hand.

Hang on—from the bone? How was that possible?

Tilda thought fast. Power could be stored in objects, and she'd felt evidence of Power in this cavern. Was stonesong the product of Power? If it was, could it be transferred to objects in the same way?

To stones ... And bones? If there *was* a link to Power ... Tilda stared into the hole. Was she much closer to a source of Power than she'd realised?

"Yanni," she said, more calmly than she felt. "I'm going to have another look in the hole, in case there *is* anything else in there."

She wriggled back inside. The music was definitely louder. Was it coming from the massive rock which had killed the miner? She stretched a hand out to touch it and her fingers brushed one of the bone fragments.

"Ow!"

She snatched her hand back. Such a pain, in her chest, when she touched the bone. Coincidence? Only one way to check. Revolted that she was about to deliberately pick up a piece of what had once been part of a living, breathing person, Tilda held her breath and grabbed a piece of the splintered bone.

Immediately the pain dragged at her chest. Except it wasn't simply a pain. Tilda recognised the intense fizz of Power, being pulled out of her centre, down her arm and into her hand. An aura—black-red—shot out of the bone and swirled around her fingers.

"Oh!" Tilda flung the bone away. The fizzing Power slammed back into her chest, and she scrambled backwards out of the hole as fast as she could. "Yanni, I think—"

Yanni was standing where she'd left him, in the middle of the cavern. A swirl of red-black light was wrapped tightly around his wrist. When he looked up at Tilda, his eyes were as black as coal.

Without thinking, Tilda swung a fist.

It connected with Yanni's jaw; his head snapped back and he dropped the bone fragment he'd been holding. Ignoring Tilda, he lunged for it.

"No!" Tilda thrust her hand out, as though she could push Yanni away from the bone in spite of the distance between them. Blue fire shot out of her fingertips and hit Yanni; he stumbled and fell heavily.

Tilda stared at her tingling fingers. Had she just used Power like a weapon? Silviu had shot red sparks at her, once, by mistake. But she had no idea how he'd done it. And she didn't know how she'd just done it, either.

"What the—?" Yanni scrambled to his feet. "What just happened?"

Tilda held up her hand in case she needed to protect herself again. A bit pointless really, as although she'd produced the blue fire a moment ago, she wasn't sure she could repeat it.

Thank Power, it looked like she didn't have to. Yanni's eyes weren't black any more.

Cautiously, Tilda lowered her arm. "The bone . . . it did something to you."

"I . . . It . . ." Yanni gulped and glanced down. "It made me feel powerful, as if I could do anything. Anything at all," he murmured.

The bone shard lay in the dirt, singing. Around it pulsed an aura, darker than the shadows it had fallen into, a sickening red-black.

"Yanni," Tilda said slowly. "I'm pretty certain there's another stone in the hole we dug the sunstone out of. And I think it might be the black ruby."

"Is this your powermage's intuition?"

"A bit more than intuition. I'm a powermage, I can *feel* Power. I can *see* it. With that . . ." Tilda waved a hand in the direction of the fallen bone. "It's different. What I can see and feel connected to that is dark, dangerous magic. Nothing at all like Power."

"So if the legend is true, and the black ruby exists, you think that some of its magic is left in those bones?" Yanni's voice had a distinct wobble in it. "And that magic affected me?" He rubbed his hand against his leg, as though that would erase the contact he'd had.

"Only while you were holding it. You feel alright now, don't you?"

Yanni nodded. "What do we do?"

These old bones, imbued with dark power, were too dangerous to leave exposed. They had to be covered up again, the mine blocked off . . .

"We need to tell Feliks, warn him. He has to close this mine. And I'll have to see Lady Duska too. No one else must find the ruby before we mages have had a chance to deal with it."

But remembering that it had taken four experienced mages *and* the Power to defeat Luisa's dark magic, Tilda couldn't help wondering if, in dealing with the black ruby, two powermages would be enough.

Chapter 19
Gloves

TILDA DIDN'T BOTHER knocking. She burst into Feliks' office, closely followed by Yanni, and started talking.

"Feliks, you have to close the mine. There's—oh! I'm sorry." Heat rose in her cheeks at the sight of Feliks' half-buttoned shirt and loose cravat.

"Come in, both of you." Feliks continued to calmly fasten the remaining buttons. "I should close the mine. Do explain why."

"It's too dangerous," Tilda began.

"Rockfalls are a hazard of the job, Tilda. The miners know that." Feliks was now tying his cravat. It looked as though he was having difficulty with the knot.

"I'm not talking about the rockfall. It's the ruby—"

"Ah, the infamous and legendary black ruby."

Feliks picked up a pair of grey leather gloves from his desk. He winced as he pulled them on, and Tilda caught sight of a curved red mark on the edge of his palm.

"It's real," she said.

"Really?" Feliks shrugged himself into the turquoise waistcoat which had been tossed carelessly onto his chair. "What makes you think that?"

"Because there are bones in the cavern as well," Tilda told him. "Arkanal's bones. There's a dark magic in them that couldn't have got into them from anything other than the ruby. And we both felt it."

Feliks' glance slid from Tilda to Yanni. "Both of you?"

Yanni nodded. "It was horrible, Feliks. I didn't feel like me any more. And all I did was hold one of the bones we found. Didn't even have to touch the ruby."

"Arkanal's black ruby." Feliks ran a long gloved finger over his lips as he walked round his desk. "A stone full of dark power. Who knows what someone might do if they found it?" His eyes darkened. "I will close the mine. For now. You two head back to Gerty's, get some rest."

Tilda shook her head. "I can't. I have to talk to Duska about this. She might know what to—"

Feliks sighed. "Tilda, it's getting late. We can talk to Lady Duska tomorrow. If the black ruby's really down that mine, it's not going anywhere for the moment. You've had a long and difficult day. A good night's sleep will make the world of difference. Go." He made a shooing movement with his gloved hand.

He might be right. Now that Tilda stopped to think about it, every inch of her body was protesting. She'd not stopped since early this morning, she'd survived a rockfall, *and* an encounter with dark power. They probably could afford to wait until tomorrow. And the thought of a bath and food and bed . . .

Feliks had already opened the office door as an invitation for her to leave; Tilda's feet moved her towards and then through the doorway. She turned to speak to Feliks.

"It will all be sorted by tomorrow," Feliks said. "You have my word." A shadow darkened his face momentarily, then he blinked and shut the door firmly in her face.

Tilda stared at the wood. Something here didn't feel right. It didn't feel right at all, but she couldn't work out why.

"We should get back to Gerty's," Yanni said. "The rest of the team'll be wondering where we are."

"All right." Tilda followed him out onto the street, but couldn't shake the feeling that she'd missed something important.

"Oi! Yanni! Where in Power have you been?" Nico was striding towards them, and he didn't look happy. "It doesn't take this long to pick up a few bags." He groaned then, seeing their empty hands. "Don't tell me they'd gone?"

"Noooo. They were there. Some still are," Yanni muttered.

"Then why haven't you—?" Nico's eyes narrowed. "Please. Tell me you didn't?"

Yanni looked anywhere but at Nico.

"You went back into the mine, didn't you?" Nico curled his hands into fists. "That blasted black ruby. Admit it, that's what you went back for, wasn't it?" He advanced on Yanni.

Yanni backed away and pointed at Tilda. "It was her idea! Not mine."

Nico focused his glare on Tilda. "Yours?"

"Yes," Tilda said. "There was stonesong and I thought maybe—"

"Stones don't sing!" Nico yelled at her.

Anger boiled up inside Tilda, hot and sharp, and words boiled up with it. "Yes they do! And you know it." She jabbed a finger at Nico. "Tomasite is really simple, but sunstone's prettier. You know that, because you heard them, that's how you knew where to dig." She raised her voice above Nico's spluttered denials. "You did, Nico! And it also means you probably also heard the odd notes down there, too. The ones that didn't fit. Didn't you?"

"It's just another stone, not a black ruby," Nico shouted. Then his eyes widened.

Tilda gasped. "Finally. You admit it."

Yanni kept looking from one to the other and back again. "Erm . . . stonesong?"

"We'll explain later." Tilda flapped her hand at him. "Nico, there is another stone in that cavern. A dangerous one. That's what we heard. I'm pretty certain it's the black ruby, and we have to make sure that no one else touches it because it changes those who come into contact with it." Out of the corner of her eye, she saw Yanni nodding violently. "That's why we've just been to see Feliks, to tell him to shut the mine down. Tomorrow, I'll tell Duska, and she and I will work out what to do next."

Nico looked puzzled. "Feliks is at the office? But he said he was going to leave as soon as he'd locked the sunstone away, had an important appointment to get to. That was a while ago. I've been back to Gerty's and come out to find you two in the time between."

"Maybe the appointment was cancelled," Tilda said. "Because he was definitely at the office a few minutes ago, getting dressed, and—" Again, there was that sense of things not being right. What reason could Feliks have had for being undressed in his office in the first place? And who put gloves on before their waistcoat? Gloves were normally the last thing you put on, after a jacket, before you went outside . . .

"Nico, I want a word with you."

Tilda spun round; Master Rosa was striding towards them.

"With me?" Nico shrugged. "What have I done?"

"You? Nothing," Rosa said, coming to a halt. She was shaking with anger. "But you can give your Master a message when you next see him. He'll regret not turning up for our . . ." Her cheeks flushed the colour of her name. "Tell him no man leaves me waiting for an hour at the Digger without good reason."

"But he was—"

Tilda kicked Yanni in the shin.

"Ow!" What did you do that for?" He glared at her.

"Sorry, foot slipped. We'll tell him," Tilda gabbled.

She grabbed Yanni by one arm, Nico by another, and walked all of them away at speed, leaving Rosa standing, bemused, on the walkway behind them.

"What did you do that for," Yanni moaned, as he limped along. "I was only going to say he was in his office."

Tilda carried on walking. "He was, but he wasn't right."

Nico pulled his arm free. "Tilda, stop. What are you on about?"

Tilda paced on the walkway as she cast her mind back. "He was . . . different. Getting dressed again . . . And then he put gloves on. Inside."

Yanni shook his head as if to clear it. "What in Power's name do Feliks' gloves have to do with anything?"

Tilda rounded on him. "He put gloves on. Inside!" She knew that was important, but why? What was she missing?

"I've known Feliks for years. He doesn't wear gloves," Nico said. "He's proud of the fact his hands aren't mine-toughened." He shoved his own hands into his pockets then, as though suddenly aware or ashamed of his own rough skin.

"Then there had to be a reason for him wearing them today. Maybe he was feeling sensitive about his scar." She frowned when she realised Yanni and Nico were staring at her. "What?"

"He doesn't have any scars," they chorused.

"Yes, he does. A curved one, right here." Tilda held out her own palm and traced a finger across it. "That beggar woman, Samya, she's got one just like it—"

An illuminorb exploded in her head.

How could she have been so stupid? There's no way two different people would have identical scars on their palms. And yet Samya and Feliks did, when the only person Tilda knew with curved scars on *her* palm was Luisa.

Luisa, who'd been branded by the Power with sections of the pattern of five silviron rings so that she couldn't hide in the future.

Tilda clenched her fist and pressed it against her mouth.

Luisa had changed her appearance before, disguised herself as the steward Freyda. Was it possible that she still had enough dark magic at her disposal to do the same again—twice? First as Samya, then as Feliks? Was she here in Pergatt, searching for the black ruby to restore her depleted powers?

Tilda whimpered.

A few minutes ago, she had told Feliks that the black ruby really existed *and* exactly where to find it.

Except it wasn't Feliks she'd told, was it?

"It's Luisa," Tilda whispered, feeling sick. "She's going to . . ." She began to run.

Nico called after her. "Tilda! Where are you going?"

She kept running. "We have to see Duska. Now!"

Chapter 20
Truth

"OPEN UP! DUSKA!" Tilda pounded on the door with both fists, willing it to open. When it did, she lost her balance and fell into the hall, landing at Sasha's feet.

Sasha gasped. "What in all Issraya is going on?"

Nico grabbed her arm. "Where's the Lady Duska?"

Sasha shook him off. "Do you mind? The Lady Duska is not here. She went out."

Tilda scrambled to her feet. "Where did she go? Sasha, this is important, we need to find her, fast."

"Well, she went out a quarter of an hour ago. With Feliks."

Every inch of Tilda's body went icy cold.

"Apparently he'd found what she was looking for, wanted to show her."

Nico frowned. "Lady Duska was after the black ruby?"

"Of course she wasn't." Tilda shook her head. "And it wasn't Feliks."

"It looked like Feliks to me," Yanni muttered.

Sasha looked at him, then at Tilda. "What's going on?"

Tilda pressed a hand to her forehead, trying to think. Luisa was after the ruby—had to be. So the Feliks-who-wasn't-actually-Feliks must be heading to the old mine. But why take Duska along? Why not go up there alone, take the stone without anyone else present to challenge its removal, and then use its dark power? Unless . . .

Was Luisa-Feliks somehow going to make use of the powermage's abilities to help locate the ruby? Worse—and here Tilda's chest tightened until she could barely breathe—was Luisa-Feliks going to lose Duska in the tunnels?

She had to stop Luisa.

Don't be stupid, a treacherous little voice whispered in Tilda's head. You're not going to be much use, are you? It took four experienced Powermages *and* the Power to beat her last time.

Oh, if only Silviu and Taimane were here, instead of in Merjan. Together, and assuming nothing dreadful happened to Duska before they reached her, four of them might have stood a chance of thwarting Luisa again while her powers were depleted.

Calling on other powermages to help was out of the question, though. Even if Tilda did manage to send a message to Merjan, and it was received in good time, it would still take days for them to reach Digdown. By then, Luisa would have the ruby in her possession and Power only knew what would have happened to Duska.

"*I'm* going to have to do this," Tilda said, the sound of her own voice startling her.

"Do what?"

"There's no time to explain, but Duska's in danger."

Sasha's face whitened.

"I'm going to try and help," Tilda reassured her, "but I'm not sure whether I can do much alone."

"You won't be alone."

She looked at Nico in surprise.

He ran a hand through his hair. "I'll come with you."

"Are you sure? Then . . . thanks," Tilda said gratefully, though worry was making it difficult to smile.

Sasha pulled Tilda towards her and hugged her fiercely. "Power be with you," she whispered, before pushing Tilda away. "Go."

"Yanni, go back to Gerty's, let them know what we're doing," Nico ordered.

"But what *are* you doing?"

"Just tell them . . ." Nico looked at Tilda. "What *do* we tell them?"

"That the black ruby's real, and we're trying to stop it falling into the wrong hands," she told them.

It was the third time in one day Tilda had climbed up to the mine; her legs protested with every step, but she kept on moving, walking as fast as her tired body could manage and breaking into jogging steps whenever the track flattened out a little. Nico kept pace with her easily—but then this was only his second trip of the day.

The third trip began to take its toll. Tilda clutched her side, trying to ignore the sharp pain in her ribs.

Nico saw and caught hold of her arm. "Rest for a moment."

"It's only . . . stitch," she panted. "We have . . . to catch . . . them up." She pulled free of him and carried on walking.

"And then what?" Nico caught her arm again and spun her round, forcing her to stop.

"Let go of me!" Tilda tried to prise his fingers off her arm and felt a familiar tingle. Before she could warn Nico, blue sparks landed on his hand.

He yelped and let go. Then he gave his hand a shake. "That hurt!"

Tilda concentrated hard, forcing the Power away from her hand until it was safely contained in her chest again, and she was fairly certain there weren't going to be any more blue sparks. "Sorry. I'm not very good at controlling it."

Nico eyed her warily. "Was that . . . Power?"

She nodded.

"And you say you can't control it?"

"Not very well," she admitted. "Except for illuminorbs. I can control them. Still learning about the rest though."

"Huh. Well, best save it for whatever we're going back to the mines for."

Tilda grimaced. "I'll try."

Nico sighed. "Tilda, I won't leave you, but I need to know what's going on. Please?"

Tilda nodded. "We ought to keep moving. I'll explain on the way."

And she did. She told Nico everything about Luisa; how she had been a contender for the Mage of Ambak years ago but was passed over for Silviu. How she'd disguised herself as the last Mage of Merjan's steward, and used Yaduvir to gain access to Ring Isle and the Power. How she'd killed Yaduvir and used dark magic to draw Power from the Ringstone. And how the mages and Power had fought back and branded her.

"That's how I recognised it was her," Tilda finished. "Because of the curved marks on both Samya and Feliks' hands."

Nico let out a low whistle. "She sounds like a right piece of work."

Tilda nodded and tried to ignore the lump of dread that had taken up residence in her stomach. "She is. And if she gets hold of Arkanal's black ruby, she'll be stronger than ever."

The dark hole of the mine entrance came into view.

"We're here," Nico said.

Tilda's steps faltered and she stopped. She had to go in, of course. But what came after that? An exploding illuminorb or a few blue sparks was all she could manage against dark magic, magic which Luisa had proved was still strong enough to maintain the disguises of two totally different people. She could always hope for another rockfall to bury Luisa, but Tilda didn't think they usually occurred to order or were selective in who they chose to crush. Maybe she should simply cross her fingers and hope that the strange stonesong she'd heard was nothing to do with the black ruby at all, but belonged to another—quite harmless—gem.

No, she was deluding herself if she thought that. She'd heard and seen enough to convince herself as to the source of that particular music.

Nico peered into the tunnel. "There are lights inside. Like the one you made after the ceiling collapse."

"Illuminorbs." Tilda's heart sank. If Duska had made them, she was using up precious Power—Power that she ought to have been saving as protection against Luisa. Except that Duska thought she was with Feliks, didn't she, and had no idea of who she was really dealing with.

"Let's go. I'll lead." Nico walked forward, Tilda close on his heels. He stepped just inside the entrance and stopped so abruptly, Tilda walked into him.

"Go on then," she said.

"I can't. Go on, I mean." Nico looked at her. "It won't let me."

"What do you mean, it won't let you?"

"There's something stopping me." Nico lifted his hand and reached out; his hand flattened against an invisible barrier. "See?" He put his shoulder to the same place and leaned his weight against thin air until he grunted with effort. It made no difference. He couldn't move any further into the tunnel.

Was this Power at work? Tilda pushed Nico out of the way and touched a wall she could not see. On contact, the unseen denseness gave way momentarily, but then pushed back against her hand, stinging her palm with the pain of a million pricking needles. She snatched her hand back. This was not something of Duska's making.

"Luisa's done this so no one else can get in." Bands of panic tightened around Tilda's chest until it hurt to breathe. "We can't get in!"

Nico stared into the tunnel. "We can't get in here—"

"I know!" Tilda wailed. "I just said that."

"But there are other tunnels." Nico turned towards her. "This Luisa woman knew this was the one we used, because she saw us using it when she was Samya. But she's not a miner. She doesn't know there are other tunnels into this old system. She won't have been able to seal them all."

There might be another way in . . . Tilda's relief was short lived as she remembered what Nico had said about the condition of the tunnels in these old mines. Her head filled with an image of rocks and soil tumbling down and she swallowed hard. "If there *are* other ways in, will they be safe?"

Nico shrugged. "I don't know. I'm not entirely sure how close they'll take us to the cavern we were digging in, either, but are you willing to take the risk? Otherwise, all we can do is sit here and wait for this . . . woman . . . to come out, try and take the ruby from her then."

They couldn't afford to wait. Luisa-Feliks was down there, and Duska was, too. Tilda would never forgive herself if something happened to the mage while she sat here waiting, doing nothing.

She took a deep breath. "We'll try another way in."

Chapter 21
Another Way In–And No Way Out

THE PEA-SIZED ORB balanced on Tilda's palm only gave out enough light to make the shadows darker as she followed Nico along narrow twisting tunnels that probably hadn't been used for centuries, but she daren't make the orb any bigger. She had to be sparing with her Power, conserve what she had left, even if she was convinced that there was a source somewhere in this mine system; there was no guarantee she could draw it to herself if she needed to. And secondly, she didn't want to announce their presence to Luisa.

"How come you know about these other tunnels?" she whispered.

"I used to come up here to explore," Nico whispered back. "I was trying to work out what I could hear in the other mines."

"You mean stonesong?" Tilda saw him nod. "Why do you hide that you can hear it?"

"Because other Masters, other miners, would be jealous. Some will do anything to remove their competition."

Anything? For the first time, Tilda realised how dangerous it might be, to have the ability to hear stonesong.

"I keep it to myself, although Yanni knows now. Perhaps I can persuade him to keep quiet about it," Nico said. "Working for Feliks has given me a chance to hone my ability, find out what different stones sound like. I've been testing myself when we work as a team, digging out decent stones and a few velvets, but one day, I'm going to be my own boss. A Master-miner, with my own team."

Tilda carefully poured a little more Power into the orb. She really didn't know how long she could continue doing this—they could be plunged into pitch black at any moment. So far, so good, though. "Aren't the Masters already suspicious of how many good stones you find?"

Nico shrugged. "I'm getting good at leading the team so it looks as though they're simply lucky and digging in the right places. Sometimes I'll ignore what I can hear so we have a poor result, and—" He stopped dead.

Tilda's heart thumped hard against her ribs. "What is it? What's wrong?" She peered over his shoulder, holding the orb higher. Ahead of them, the tunnel split, branching off into deeper darkness.

"I think it's this way." Nico pointed to the right.

"Wait."

There was a sensation . . . a gentle pull on Tilda's core. She hadn't noticed it when she was walking—perhaps she'd only noticed it now because she'd stopped. It was faint, but it was definitely there. "We have to go that way." She pointed at the left hand tunnel.

"It's not, it's that one."

"Look, I know you're the miner, but I'm the mage." She was, wasn't she? She had abilities of her own, and it was time to use them. "I can feel the Power. Sometimes it pulls me to where it is or where it needs me to be. Right now, it's pulling me. That way." Tilda pointed again, hoping that she'd sounded sure enough for Nico to believe her.

Nico sucked at his bottom lip. "Are you sure?"

"Yes." She held Nico's gaze as he studied her.

Nico looked away first. "Like you said, you're the mage. We'll go that way, although it doesn't look very wide. Might get even narrower."

"If we get to the point where we can't go any further, we'll come back and try the other tunnel, however much the Power's pulling me," Tilda promised.

Nico nodded and stepped to one side. "Agreed. Lead on, then."

As Tilda walked ahead with the light, she saw that Nico was right— the tunnel was barely wide enough for one person, and narrowed in some places to such an extent that she was forced to turn sideways and walk crab-wise. She'd just squeezed herself between two rocks at one of the tightest points yet, when the tunnel opened up a little.

"Thank Power, it's getting easier," she told Nico in a whisper.

A sharp crack echoed from somewhere nearby, followed by the unmistakeable rattle of falling stones.

Fear rose up from the soles of Tilda's boots and settled in her chest. Not again . . . She turned her head, searching for Nico. "Rockfall?"

Another crack, another rattle, the echoes dying away.

Nico frowned. "I don't think so. Didn't sound big enough." As he spoke, the sound came for a third time. "And it's happening too regularly."

Tilda swallowed hard. "Carry on, then?"

Nico nodded. "But keep the noise down. It could be your Luisa."

Oh, how she wished he hadn't said that. She'd have to actually *do* something if he was right . . . and she had no idea what that something might be. She crept down the tunnel, barely daring to breathe, and turned a corner.

Ahead of her, the tunnel came to a rocky dead end; a rocky dead end with a thin sliver of light shining from it. Tilda let the orb wink out and pressed herself into the tunnel wall.

"Are you sure this is the right place, Feliks?" Duska's voice echoed down to where Tilda stood.

"I was told the ruby must be in the cavern, but not its exact location."

That was Feliks. Rather, it was Luisa *posing* as Feliks, Tilda reminded herself.

"And you're sure Tilda wasn't too badly hurt?"

What? Duska thought Tilda had been hurt? No wonder she'd overcome her terrible fear of the dark to come down into the mine at Feliks' bidding. She'd be wanting to recover the ruby and make certain it couldn't hurt anyone else.

"I'm sure."

A shadow moved across the sliver of light, and everything went black for a moment before the light returned.

"Well, if the ruby's here, it's well hidden. All we've found so far is sunstone."

Tilda grabbed Nico and pulled him close so she could whisper into his ear. "The cavern—it's on the other side of this rock."

She had to see if there was a way into it. But the closer Tilda got to the crack in the rock where the light spilled through, the tighter the walls pressed in on her, even worse than the thinnest parts of the tunnel. Rocks snagged Tilda's jacket and scraped her exposed skin, but she kept pulling and wriggling herself closer to the light until she was firmly wedged and simply couldn't move any more.

From her new—uncomfortable—position, Tilda could see that the light came through a crack in the rocks. It was the width of two fingers, and the length of two hands. No way into the cavern through here, but if she could see what was happening—

"Explogravitas," Duska said.

Another crack—the closest yet—almost deafened Tilda and she recoiled, her ears ringing.

"It is a good job that you are as adept at breaking the rock as you are, Lady Duska," Luisa-Feliks said.

"It's surprising how much you can focus when you don't like being underground."

Into the silence which followed fell the sound of several odd musical notes.

Tilda clapped a hand over her mouth to prevent her shout of surprise from escaping. She managed to turn her head to look for Nico; the thin strip of light showed him wedged much further back in the tunnel, unable to get any closer to her. His eyes were wide.

Taking her hand from her mouth, Tilda pointed at Nico, then at her ears; he nodded. So he could hear it too. It had to be Arkanal's ruby.

Carefully, Tilda shifted position slightly until she could see through the crack in the rock. The slice of cavern that was visible looked as though it was being lit by a mixture of candle stubs fixed to the rocks, and floating orbs.

"And what have we here?" Feliks' voice.

A shadow darkened the crack and Tilda jerked her head away, banging it on the rock close behind. She bit back a cry of pain and blinked away the tears that sprang into her eyes. Then she leaned forward again. If she twisted a bit more, like so, she could angle her face . . .

She was rewarded first with the sight of a jacket sleeve, and then, as she shifted ever so slightly again, a gloved hand reaching deep into a hole much larger than any she remembered the team digging.

Another shadow crossed in front of the crack. Was that Duska?

"Is that a skeleton?"

"I do believe it is, my Lady. I think your little blasts have broken the rock enough to uncover Arkanal, the miner of legend. And unless I'm much mistaken . . ."

The burst of strange music was almost deafening. If Tilda had had room, she'd have pressed her hands against her ears. As it was, she could only watch as the gloved hand withdrew from the hole, holding a lump of red-black stone.

"The infamous black ruby."

"Thank Power we found it," Duska said. "We'd best get it out of here. I'll keep it safe until I return to Ring Isle."

Through the crack, Tilda saw a second hand reaching towards the first, and then Feliks' voice dripped like poison into her ears.

"Whatever made you think I'd be handing the ruby over to you for safe keeping, my Lady?"

"But I thought . . ." A hard edge crept into Duska's voice. "Feliks, you can't possibly be considering keeping it?"

"Why not?"

Tilda saw another gloved hand make a complicated motion and opened her mouth to shout a warning. Except she didn't make a sound. She clutched her throat as a flash of green light from the cavern seared across her eyes, leaving her blinking pink spots.

Duska must have realised something was wrong, was fighting for the ruby!

"Shadarthred capturi," Feliks said.

Something blacker than black shot across the light. Tilda didn't have to see now, to know what had been aimed at Duska; the blackness would open up like a net and seize her.

An answering fizzle of green sparks, then a thump as something soft hit the ground.

"Ah, I see in your eyes, that you begin to suspect . . . Perhaps now is the time to remove this tiresome disguise." Feliks' voice changed as he spoke, growing higher, lighter, until it took on the characteristics of a voice Tilda had heard before. Still did, sometimes, in her nightmares.

Luisa.

Tilda twisted her head this way and that, trying to see. The cavern was darker now, only the candles left alight, all the illuminorbs gone. Her stomach twisted then as much as her head. No illuminorbs—did that mean Duska had used up too much of her Power so she couldn't keep them lit? Was she hurt? Icy cold dread ran down Tilda's spine. Was Duska . . . dead?

A burst of brilliant white lit up the cavern, blinding Tilda. A burst of laughter followed.

"It grants me its power already," Luisa crooned. "One mage alone is no match . . . You were so easily overcome, Lady Duska. I wonder, did all that rock blasting use up most of your Power? Producing so many illuminorbs couldn't have helped either, yet I'd have expected you to have more Power at your disposal than that. Perhaps the Power, divided between five mages, is not as strong as I had feared. If this is all it takes to deplete you, I imagine the other four will be no problem either. Tell me, shall I go after the little one, Tilda, first?"

Hearing her name, Tilda shivered.

Luisa carried on talking. "No, perhaps not. She won't have been trained yet, she'll be no fun at all. It will be like stamping on a marsh beetle."

Tilda held her breath as a woman moved to stand in front of the crack. Patterns of red-black light danced and writhed across her exposed skin, and even the brilliant light now illuminating the cavern couldn't quite hide the purple-black aura filling the air immediately around her body.

Luisa was standing within touching distance on the other side of the rock.

And Tilda couldn't do a single thing about it.

"I promise the ruby will be kept quite safe, by the way," Luisa continued, a steely note creeping into her voice. "And when I have discovered the full reach of its magic and power, I will use it to destroy the powermages and take Issraya for my own, as I always intended. Especially as there will shortly be only four mages left to defeat."

Only four? What was Luisa planning to do to Duska? Tilda fought back a wave of nausea.

"You look confused, my Lady." Luisa dropped down, below Tilda's eye level—she must be squatting beside Duska—and her voice drifted up through the crack. "The tunnel's going to collapse, you see. And no one will realise the Lady Duska was even here, until perhaps they dig up her bones in years to come. Mind, you're in good company, Arkanal's lying right beside you."

This couldn't be happening.

Tilda dug her nails into her palms, using the pain to break through the fear and helplessness threatening to overwhelm her. She was so close, yet not near enough. She couldn't use her Power. Couldn't help Duska. Couldn't stop Luisa leaving with the black ruby.

She was next to useless.

Luisa rose quickly to her feet and moved out of Tilda's view.

"Explogravita completimen giganta!"

There was an almighty crash from the cavern; everything went black. The rocks which Tilda had been so tightly wedged between gave way and she fell with them, mercifully landing on rather than under the stones. Grittiness coated her skin, caught in her throat, and set her coughing.

"Illiminarka spherus," she gasped. Her voice was back—Luisa's enchantment of silence had broken.

The orb's light was hazy, dulled by the cloud of dust filling the ruined cavern. Tons of stone and earth now blocked the tunnel; its entrance and half a wall had collapsed, enlarging the hole where Nico's team had so recently dug for the sunstone. Apart from where Tilda had fallen, the rest of the floor was relatively clear, except for over there, where under a layer of black, dust-covered ropes, lay—

"Duska!"

Tilda barely registered that the orb she'd created rose up from her palm and floated above her head as she scrambled towards Duska and tore frantically at the ropes still wrapped around her body. Was the shadow thread enchantment broken too?

"Duska, can you hear me? Duska, please, open your eyes."

The ropes disintegrated and gave way, but Duska lay pale and unresponsive, even when freed from what had bound her and with Tilda shaking her shoulder.

Power forbid, was she dead? No, her chest was still rising and falling with shallow breaths.

"Tilda, I can't get through."

Tilda stopped shaking Duska and looked up.

There was a Tilda-sized hole where she'd fallen into the cavern. A Tilda-sized hole, not a Nico-sized one. That hadn't stopped Nico trying to squeeze through it, even though it was obvious he wasn't going to succeed. If he couldn't get into the cavern—Tilda glanced down—there was no hope of getting Duska out.

She left Duska's side and scrambled over to Nico. "We can make the hole bigger."

Nico sagged, held up only by the stones he was fighting to get past. "No tools. It'll be easier to go back, get help."

Tilda nodded. But who could they ask? Nico's team was down to only three fit members, and it would take time they couldn't afford to bring another team of miners down here again—they'd have to ask another Master for permission first. Isaak or Sasha wouldn't be much help, and the other mages were hundreds of miles away. They'd know what to do. If only it was possible to contact them . . .

Maybe it was.

Duska's door in the forest—why hadn't she remembered it earlier? It had been locked and unlocked using the Power stored in the key, combined with the incantation. If it still opened without Duska speaking the words and holding the key . . . It had to be worth a try.

Tilda dredged her memory for the words she'd heard spoken, back in Georj's strong room . . . Dreytall Pergatt . . . Dretambra Pergatt . . . no, neither of those were right. But it was something like that . . .

"Drethtallambra Pergatt!" Yes, that was it.

With a whispered apology to the unconscious Duska, Tilda felt inside the mage's collar and pulled on the chain. When the key appeared at the end of it, Tilda gave a sharp tug—no time to undo the clasp—and the chain snapped. She passed chain and key up to Nico.

"Go back to Digdown and keep this safe. Find Isaak at Duska's house, tell him I order him to take you to the door in the woods. When you get there, hold the key against the circle of rings above the handle and say 'Drethtallambra Perga—No!'" She shook her head. "No, saying Pergatt brought us here. Try . . ." She thought fast. "Merjan. Yes, say Drethtellambra Merjan. Got that?"

"Drethambra Mer—"

"No! Dretht-*all*-ambra Merjan"

"Dretht-*all*-ambra Merjan," Nico repeated. "Right. Got it. Dretht-*all*-ambra Merjan. And hold this close to the rings?"

Tilda nodded. "That's it. A keyhole will appear. Use that key to unlock the door and when you go through, you'll be in Merjan City, in Gemsman Georj's strong room. You might have to bang on the door until he lets you out, because I don't know how it works on the return trip. Isaak might. Then find Silviu and Taimane, they were going to the Historykeepers. Tell them Luisa's attacked Duska and she's hurt. Bring them through the door again as fast as you can." Power, she hoped he would remember all of this.

Nico looked at her, a frown creasing his brow. "What if it doesn't work?"

"The door? I don't know. Write a note and try pushing it under?" Tilda shrugged. "If it doesn't work, just . . . come back and dig me and Duska out. Then we'll decide what to do next."

"Will you be all right?"

Tilda felt her mouth move. She hoped it looked like a smile, rather than the grimace she was trying to suppress. "I'll be fine. Luisa's not going to come back through that lot, is she?" She tried to keep her voice sounding cheerful. "You'll need light. Here, take one of the candles."

She prised one of the larger candle stubs free of the rocks and tested her Power level. She'd not tried this before, but as the illuminorb was still bright above her head, she was willing to give it a go. Pulling gently on her Power, she willed it into her index finger and shot one tiny blue spark onto the wick; it caught and burned brightly. Shielding the flame, she passed the candle through the crack to Nico. "Don't get lost."

He took the candle, then grabbed Tilda's hand and squeezed it. "I'll be back as soon as I can."

Sudden and unexpected fear closed a tight hand around Tilda's throat. She nodded, unable to say a word. Then she watched as Nico and the candlelight got smaller and disappeared into the darkness.

Chapter 22
Playing with Power

TILDA LOWERED HERSELF down next to Duska. Gently, she checked for a pulse and was relieved to feel one, beating slowly, but still beating. What had Luisa done, to keep the mage so still and pale? Would the effects wear off? Or was Duska destined to lie like this, forever sleeping?

"Silviu would know what to do, I'm sure," Tilda whispered to Duska. "But for now, I'm here, and I won't leave you until Nico comes back for us."

Feeling more alone than she'd ever felt in her life, she couldn't keep a brave face on any longer. She laid her head on her knees and wept.

This was all her fault. If she'd not had the crazy idea of pretending to find out about Pergatt's mining history and coming down the mine with Nico's team, she'd never have discovered she could hear stonesong. She'd never have heard the music of the black ruby or come back to the mine to find it. Duska wouldn't be lying here now if she'd not run straight to Feliks to tell him that the ruby existed— she should've gone to Duska first, not him. Especially when it wasn't even Feliks she'd told, but Luisa in disguise. She'd even missed the most obvious warning sign that the Power had left branded onto Luisa.

Silviu was going to be so disappointed with her. Tilda could just imagine the look on his face when she had to admit that the only thing she'd done right in Pergatt was create a few orbs and maintain their light. She lifted her head and stared at the orb floating near the ceiling.

Still floating. Still brightly lit.

Tilda sniffed and wiped her nose on her sleeve. Then she wiped her cheeks dry. How was the orb doing that? She certainly wasn't making it happen—not consciously, anyway. And inside . . . her Power didn't feel depleted at all. It was still there, fizzing away.

Not for the first time, she wondered if there was Power in the mine that she was managing to draw to her without realising. There'd been that mention of earthdraws, back on Ring Isle, but Tilda couldn't imagine that it just . . . happened. Power must need *some* effort to pull it into a mage, surely?

She sat up straighter. She'd seen the effect that drawing Power could have on the powermages when they were injured or drained; it healed and strengthened them. If she still had Power, could she transfer some of it to Duska? Silviu would disapprove of that too, no doubt, especially when he'd not taught her how to do it, but—

"Silviu's not here," Tilda told herself. "He won't know." She looked down at Duska; in the mage's current state, not even she would know.

She pushed herself onto her knees, picked up Duska's limp hand, and held it tight. She might end up draining herself of Power, but she'd rather chance that and face dying herself, than hold onto her own portion and do nothing at all.

But how to make the transfer? Was it enough to rely on gut feeling? She squared her shoulders and took a deep breath; she was about to find out.

Tilda shut her eyes and tuned into her Power. Its familiar fizz filled her chest, full of energy. She would have to be careful with this, especially if she didn't know exactly what Luisa had done to Duska. Too much Power might make things worse. She had to make the Power less energetic, so it wouldn't be too much of a shock to an injured mage . . .

She imagined pressing down, calming the energy until the fizz was barely noticeable. Only then did she draw her Power into her hand. It felt different—softer, gentler—and instead of focusing it into the familiar shape of an orb, Tilda imagined it seeping slowly from her pores, coating Duska's hand like a syrup before being absorbed into her skin.

After a few minutes, Tilda stopped the imagined flow and opened her eyes. She let out a breath, feeling strangely tired, but still able to detect the fizz of her portion inside her. Had she used any of her Power at all? Achieved anything? She studied Duska's face. Perhaps it was her imagination, but there seemed to be a little more colour in the unconscious mage's cheeks.

Difficult to tell in the light of just one illuminorb.

An orb sprang to life above Tilda's head. Without any extra effort or direction on her part, it floated up to join the first and added its brightness to the cavern.

Able to see more, Tilda gasped. Yes, Duska was definitely less pale. And her breathing seemed to be less ragged, too.

Tilda let go of Duska's hand and sat back on her heels, relieved and secretly rather pleased. She'd made a difference, thank Power. And it seemed as though formal lessons weren't the only way to learn how to control and use the Power. Why hadn't Silviu told her from the start that there was an element of intuition, of feeling how best to use it in any given circumstance? Look at that last orb; she'd barely had to think about her need for it, and it had appeared.

Or had that been a fluke? Could she really think them into existence? A flash of thought, and a third, smaller light appeared. Then a larger, and soon there were a dozen or more different sized lights bobbing near the ceiling. The cavern felt as though it was bathed in daylight—and Tilda couldn't detect much effect on her Power at all. It continued to fizz in the way she was used to.

Tilda stared up at the balls of light, wondering if they were fixed in place. She pushed herself to her feet and reached for one of the lowest orbs, but drew her hand back without touching it. What if it exploded in the cavern? If it did, she needed to hope there'd be nothing worse than a shower of blue sparks and a singed sleeve again. A tentative prod knocked the light out of place and it wobbled for a moment before settling in its new position.

Tilda grinned. This was going to be fun.

She didn't know how long she played with the orbs, arranging and rearranging them into different patterns, but eventually she tired of the game. As a grand finale, she pushed all the orbs together into one big clump. Combined, they were like a miniature sun, forcing her to squint against their light.

Power, it was so bright, even the rocks seemed to be shining. That patch over there, roughly where they'd dug up the tomasite and jennisine, was glinting the brightest of all, the rock tinged with green.

Tilda's heart gave a massive thump against her ribs. "Extellerinq," she whispered.

Heavy, pressing dark closed in on her as every orb winked out simultaneously.

And there, in the blackness, as she stared at the place where she knew the hole was, a faint glow appeared. A green glow. And within it, a paler stripe in the rock sparkled green.

Was it another stone? Couldn't be—stones had to be cut and polished to sparkle that much. And there was no stonesong—the cavern was silent apart from the sound of Tilda's and Duska's breathing.

Then . . . Tilda barely dared to voice the thought. Had she found the source of her apparently unlimited ability to produce illuminorbs?

She spoke another orb into being—only a small one, but plenty big enough to show where she was putting her feet. Slowly she approached the glow; there was only one way to be sure.

As soon as her fingers brushed the green light, Tilda knew exactly why Duska had described the Pergattian portion of Power as something that danced. It was as though someone was playing piano with their fingers over Tilda's skin. There was a pattern to it, a lightness, an underlying tickle of joy. She reached further into the coloured aura, and touched the glittering stripe in the rock.

As soon as she made contact with the substance, the green light flared and wrapped itself around her wrist.

Then a narrow wisp of blue joined it.

You've found it, Tilda!

"Found what?" Tilda's voice echoed loudly in the cavern.

Fallen starmetal . . . Tilda, you've found the silviron. You have found all of us . . .

Three more wisps of colour shot out from the silviron. Yellow for Kradlock, purple for Nargan, the familiar red of Ambak—all writhing and twisting between the thick strand of Pergattian green and Tilda's own Merjanian blue, forming a bracelet of coloured light around her wrist.

A chorus of different voices filled Tilda's head. *Well done, Tilda.*

All five portions . . . No, this musn't happen! No mage could be in contact with all five strands at the same time—it wasn't allowed, would destroy her!

Tilda gasped and tried to tug her hand away as the fizzing of Power in her chest grew in intensity, spreading along her arms right to the ends of her fingertips. It ran down her legs and into her toes. It even flooded her scalp until she was sure her hair must be standing on end. The Power filled every part of her, building in pressure, and just when she thought she couldn't take any more—would burst with it—the connection broke. The auras unwrapped themselves and shrank quickly back towards the silviron. The blue strand lingered a moment or two longer around Tilda's fingers than the others. It was like swirling her hand in warm water.

We will meet again on Ring Isle, Tilda.

And then all the colours were gone. The only thing left behind was a line of silver-grey metal, sparkling in the light of a small illuminorb, and buried deep in the rock.

Chapter 23

Rescue

SHE SHOULDN'T HAVE touched the silviron.

Tilda scrubbed at her arms, trying to rub away the painful tingling that filled every inch of her skin. It must be dangerous, to be so full of Power? She'd been touched by all five portions at once—she shuddered, remembering what had happened to Luisa when she'd done the same thing.

In a panic, Tilda inspected her wrist, but there weren't any marks visible; the Power hadn't chosen to brand her like it had Luisa. Was that because the portions had come to her of their own choosing? Whatever their reason for doing so, she didn't want this much Power inside her. It hurt too much. She had to rid herself of it, or she'd explode.

She sent an illuminorb shooting up towards the ceiling, but it didn't bring any relief. On the verge of producing another, Tilda stopped and forced herself to think.

If all five portions had come to her through the silviron and filled her with Power without her asking for it, they must have had a good reason for doing so. Did they need her to use the Power they'd granted her? If they did, it was probably for something more important than making balls of light. Tilda looked up, guiltily. Two would be enough. They gave plenty of light, she didn't need more. Perhaps she ought to use the Power to magic up food and drink instead? She had no idea how long she'd been down here, but it was definitely hours since she'd eaten anything and her throat was parched. No, she couldn't be selfish. She ought to give Duska more, or concentrate on getting them both out of this cavern.

Now she thought about it, getting out sounded like the better option. Tilda had witnessed Duska using Power to smash rocks. She could even remember the incantation: explogravitas. If she did the same thing to the rocks blocking the main tunnel, then help might arrive more quickly. And maybe she'd finally get to eat the hot chicken pie and drink the cool, fresh water she was so looking forward to . . .

Even with her course of action decided, Tilda hesitated. This was another lesson she was going to have to learn on her own. Hopefully she wouldn't make too many mistakes.

She connected with the Power in an instant, the fizzing almost eager to be set free. She opened up an imaginary channel and sent it rushing down her arm, willing its intensity into her index finger. Then she held the Power there, keeping it firmly in place until she had selected one of the rocks blocking the entrance.

When she'd chosen one that didn't look too big, she pointed at it. "Explogravitas," she said, and let the Power go.

A thin line of five-stranded light shot out of her finger end; the rock exploded into dust with a sharp cracking sound.

"Oh!" Tilda looked at her finger. She had half expected to see a hole where the Power had emerged, or a telltale glow, but there was nothing.

She eyed up the blockage at the tunnel entrance. There were a lot of rocks. Even if she got through them all with the Power currently at her disposal, would she be able to break through Luisa's invisible barrier too? She'd forgotten about that. Maybe she ought to focus on where she'd fallen into the cavern instead, especially if there was a chance Nico was going to come back that way. She blasted another rock at the entrance into oblivion anyway. It was extremely satisfying.

But something niggled at her, something to do with using the Power in this way. She was able to break rocks, but why did doing that to clear her escape route feel wrong? Was she supposed to use the Power for another reason?

Tilda turned her head slowly and stared at the strip of silviron glinting in the stone.

She could break rock.

And in that moment, everything made sense. What was the point of wasting the Power she'd been given by the portions, when she had every faith that Nico would arrive at some point with help, to dig her and Duska out? She might have to wait longer to see daylight, but while she waited . . .

"The Power needs me to get the silviron out," she said, her voice loud in the cavern.

Ignoring her thirst and hunger, Tilda set to work. She experimented, working on rock a little way from the starmetal, until she was confident she could control the amount of Power needed to turn a small, measured section of rock into dust. Slowly, carefully, she worked around the edges of the silviron, exposing more and more of it.

Eventually, the Power started running out. Instead of the energetic fizz she'd experienced just after the five portions had connected with her, all Tilda could feel now was the faintest of tingles between blasts. Added to which, her body was aching, her fingers felt raw, and tears kept filling her eyes. She blinked them away in frustration, because the silviron was still not free. How could she have wasted Power creating orbs and breaking those rocks at the entrance? She should have realised sooner what the Power intended her to achieve with it.

Well, she'd drain herself before she gave up on getting the silviron out. While there was still a little bit of fizz left in her . . .

She dredged up every last scrap of Power she could feel, aimed, and released it, staggering slightly as it left her finger. There was no more; she was completely empty.

The rock she'd targeted disintegrated, and the silviron shifted slightly, tipping forward.

Tilda sucked in a breath. Had she done it? Blasted away enough rock to let the silviron fall out?

It seemed not. The silviron remained stubbornly in place.

Tilda groaned. "No. You have to come free, you have to." She staggered across the cavern and grabbed the exposed edges of the starmetal, ignoring the slivers of rock stuck to its surface which sliced into her hands. She pulled and pulled, but without Power and weak from lack of food and drink, her efforts were fruitless. What little strength she had left faded quickly away, until she was left clutching the silviron and panting.

"Come on, dammit!"

With the very last of her strength, she heaved on the starmetal, knowing that it still wouldn't be enough.

A moment of resistance—then the silviron slipped smoothly from its millennia-old rocky prison.

Tilda fell backwards. She lay on the floor, panting, hardly daring to believe what had just happened. Slowly she sat up and looked at what she held in her hands.

The chunk of silviron filled her palm and sparkled in the light of the illuminorbs which still glowed softly over Tilda's head. She ran her fingers over the surface of the starmetal; it was cool to the touch, most of it ridged and rounded like a lump of melted wax, but pressed thin and sharp on one side—the side that had caught her eye initially. And it had a song . . .

The music flooded over Tilda, and she closed her eyes to drink it in. Silviron had a song—a song made up of silvery, liquid notes. Notes that cascaded over each other, lifting her weary spirits. She raised the silviron to her ear to hear it better.

Her eyes shot open and she frowned. The music wasn't coming from the metal.

She stared at the silviron, then at the hole she'd pulled it from. If the silviron *had* had this song, she should have heard it well before it was fully exposed, but she hadn't. She'd only heard the music when the silviron had come free. From her brief mining experience, she knew that stonesong could be heard before the stones were dug up—that's how Nico found them, after all. Yet there hadn't been a single note of music in the cavern since the moment Luisa had taken the black ruby and collapsed the tunnel—until now.

Doubt crept into Tilda's mind as she stared down at the silviron again. If it wasn't silviron's song, then . . .

She tore her eyes away from the metal and looked back at the hole in the rock. Deep in its shadow, a lump of pale stone gleamed. So it *was* stonesong, after all. Tilda leaned closer, and the music's volume increased. The silviron must have blocked it somehow.

Holding the silviron carefully in one hand, Tilda reached for the pale stone with the other.

As her fingers closed around it and she pulled it towards her, there was a sound behind her—the scraping of stone on stone. Tilda spun round, and watched, open-mouthed, as the rocks blocking the tunnel entrance gave a great heave and then parted. In the new opening was someone Tilda had no difficulty in recognising, and she'd never been so glad to see him in her life.

"I see you've mastered illuminorbs," Silviu said.

Before Tilda could answer, she heard a groan. She shoved the lump of silviron into one pocket, the stone into the other, and scrambled over to Duska. The mage stirred feebly and then became still once more.

"Duska?" Silviu clambered through the hole and knelt at Tilda's side. "What happened?"

"Shadow threads," she told him.

Silviu swore under his breath. "Bring the stretcher."

Stretcher? What stretcher? Who was he talking to?

"Got it."

Nico! Here, and holding a roll of canvas with two poles sticking out of it. And Yanni and Timo scrambling towards her, and—Power, only just climbing through the hole from the tunnel . . . was that Isaak?

"You came back," Tilda whispered.

"Course." Nico nodded towards Silviu as he unrolled the stretcher. "He made short work of that invisible barrier at the entrance, then it was easy to lead him down here with the others. Knew it'd take more than two of us to get the Lady Duska out if she was hurt bad."

When the barely conscious Duska had been comfortably settled on the stretcher, Silviu took one of the handles. Isaak, Timo, and Yanni took hold of the others.

"Lift," Silviu ordered. "Nico, you go in front with Tilda."

It wasn't long before Tilda found herself outside the mine. Fresh air, at last. She threw her head back and breathed deeply. She'd never been so glad to see the moon before, either; she stared up at the thin sliver of brightness hanging in the dark sky. It had been dusk when she and Nico had entered the mine.

"How long have I been underground?"

"A little over twenty four hours," Nico said.

She'd been down there for a night and a day, and now it was night again? Power, no wonder she was exhausted, even without being drained of Power. She'd had no idea—it hadn't felt that long, but then time played tricks sometimes. She knew time slowed down sometimes outside of contact with the Ringstone. Maybe this time, time had sped up outside it and slowed within. She couldn't imagine how she'd kept going for so long without sustenance, unless the Power had had something to do with that, as well.

There was still so much she didn't understand about what was possible with the Power.

There'd be a chance to ask about it directly from her portion though, once the Ringstone was repaired. The silviron was reassuringly heavy in her pocket, and with a jolt, Tilda realised that she'd not told Silviu about finding it yet. Probably best not to, either. At least until they got Duska home and were somewhere more private.

And what of the white stone with the beautiful stonesong? She'd not mentioned that, either. Nico might be interested in seeing it;

in fact, he could even have it if he liked. Tilda would be happy just remembering its music . . .

"Nico, I found this. Do you want it?" She fished the stone out of her pocket and held it out to him.

Nico took it and gave it a quick glance. Then he did a double take. "Power in perpetuity! Tilda, it's a diamant, worth fifty marks at least."

Power, she hadn't expected that. "A diamant?" Nico nodded, and would've handed it back, but Tilda shook her head. "You keep it."

"What? I can't, it's far too valuable." Nico thrust the stone at her again. "I—"

"I don't want it. Keep it, please." Gently, she pushed his hand away. "I've got silviron."

"Silviron. The stuff in the Ringstone? You found some of that, too?"

Tilda nodded. Power, but she was tired. Did she have the energy to explain? "It's what we came here looking for, why we asked for your team. Feliks knew what we were really after, but we couldn't risk anyone else finding out," she said, seeing a flash of hurt cross his features.

"You didn't trust me?"

"Not at first," Tilda admitted. "But I do now. I trusted you with my life when you left me in that cavern. That's why you can have the diamant. Consider it a thank you, for coming back for me."

Nico rolled the diamant in his hand. Then he slipped it into his own pocket. "In that case, I'll be glad to accept it. Might even be enough to set me up as a Master."

"Good." Tilda stumbled and would have fallen, but Nico caught her arm.

"No more talk. Keep walking, let's get you home."

Chapter 24

Revelation

HOME THIS TIME meant Duska's house, not Gerty's. To Tilda's immense relief, Duska had come to her senses enough on the way down from the mine to be able to walk into her home. When she was safely inside, with Sasha and Isaak helping her to her room, Silviu dismissed the miners, leaving Tilda to see them out.

Nico paused on the step. "Will you send a message to Gerty's tomorrow, let us know how the Lady Duska's doing?"

"Course. I'm sure Silviu will know what to do to help her recover quickly. Now go, rest. You deserve it." Tilda yawned. "I need to sleep, too. Goodnight." She closed the door and joined Silviu in the parlour, where she sank gratefully onto a chair. Who cared if she made it dusty? She needed a bath. But first, she had to know . . . "When do we go after Luisa?"

Silviu stopped pacing. "We don't."

"Why not? She's got the black ruby, will draw on its magic and do awful things. She'll—"

"There's no point, Tilda." Silviu steepled his fingers and briefly touched them to his lips. "Thanks to you, we've been warned in good time. Even with the ruby in Luisa's possession, it will take days until she can reach Merjan, longer still to get to Ring Isle. Assuming that's what she intends to do, of course. She may lay low for a while instead, plan her next move carefully. We have time to spare, and you and Duska need a day or two's rest before you are fit to travel."

Tilda didn't want to think about Luisa getting away with the ruby, but with Duska still weakened by the shadow threads, Silviu was probably right to wait.

And she couldn't deny that the effects of the last few days were beginning to make themselves felt. Her own body was one enormous ache with no beginning or end. Hunger gnawed deep in her stomach. Her lips were dry and cracked, and she had no Power left that she could detect.

No Power—which was fatal.

Tilda sat up quickly. "Silviu, I used all my Power!"

"You drained yourself?" Silviu was at her side in an instant.

"Yes . . ." She looked up at him, fear filling the space inside her chest where the Power used to fizz. "How long . . . until . . . ?"

Silviu laid his hand over hers. "Don't worry, the consequences are not immediate. Taimane forgot to mention that, didn't he? I'll give you a little of mine, keep you going. Not too much, mind. I don't want to drain myself, either."

Tilda nodded and leaned her head back against the chair as the comforting warmth of Ambak's portion seeped into her aching body. "Oh, that's better. I can't believe I used all the extra Power I drew in the mine, making orbs and blasting the rocks. Ow!"

Silviu's grip suddenly tightened, his fingers digging into her collarbone. "You drew Power in the mine and then broke rocks with it? On your own?"

Tilda felt her bottom lip wobble. "I know you said I shouldn't, but it was an accident. I didn't mean to draw, honest. It just happened when I touched the silviron. I promise I didn't waste it. I used it to get the silviron out. I thought I was doing the right thing," she finished miserably.

Silviu crouched down in front of the chair. He gripped its arms, keeping Tilda pinned in her seat. His pale eyes bored into her. "Silviron?"

"Oh!" Tilda fumbled inside her jacket pocket. "Sorry, I forgot."

Silviu's gaze dropped from Tilda's face to what she was holding out to him. "You found it."

"Yes. Take it. There's no Power actually in it, though."

Silviu took the silviron from Tilda with something akin to reverence. Then he hauled her towards him and almost crushed her in a one-armed hug.

"Matilda Benjasson, you are a marvel," he whispered, and let go.

Released, Tilda dropped back into the chair and sucked in a breath to replace the one Silviu had squeezed out of her. "You don't mind?"

"How can I mind, when you have discovered what both I and Taimane didn't really believe existed?" He stared down at the precious object in his hand. "With this . . ." He shook his head, apparently lost for words. Abruptly, he stood. "We can repair the Ringstone now, and it must be done without delay. We leave tomorrow for Merjan City."

"You've got no chance of leaving tomorrow," Sasha said. She'd entered the parlour without either of them hearing. "Lady Duska's in no fit state, sir, and Tilda doesn't look much better. Excuse me." Politely but firmly, she elbowed Silviu out of the way and set the tray she was carrying on Tilda's lap.

Aromatic steam tickled Tilda's nose and her stomach growled. "Thank you, Sasha." She picked up the spoon and dipped it into the bowl of broth. "Silviu's right, though. We have to go back, as soon as we can. I'll manage, and so will Duska, once she understands why. I'm sure she'd want to travel. Even if she is feeling rough. "

"Rough?" Sasha snapped. "She's almost done for. It's madness to move her yet."

"But move her, we must." Silviu's tone did not invite argument. "Do all you can to make Duska comfortable for the moment, and we will leave in the morning, at eight bells. I assume you have spare rooms for myself and Tilda, Sasha? Good. Tilda, eat, bathe, and grab a few hours of sleep, in that order."

Power, but this broth was good! Tilda took another mouthful, and nearly choked on it as what Silviu had said filtered through to her tired brain. If they left at eight bells, she wouldn't have time to see Nico or the team before she left Digdown. She had to say goodbye. She swallowed the soup quickly. "Silviu, I have to see Nico and his team before we leave."

"I'm not sure there will be time. They will understand our need for urgency, I'm sure."

"Please?" Exhaustion and disappointment brought tears to Tilda's eyes. "It won't take long."

Silviu crossed his arms. "It means that much to you?"

She nodded. "They looked after me . . ."

"Very well. I shall send Isaak to them with a message. But we leave at eight bells, whether you have seen them or not. Understood?"

"Yes. Thank you." Tilda leaned back in the chair, too tired now even to lift the spoon. Her body had simply shut down—she didn't know how she was going to manage a bath, but she must, before she climbed into bed.

And then, there was nothing else to do but sleep, until tomorrow morning.

Thank Power.

Chapter 25
Presents From a Friend

FELIKS' ENTIRE TEAM were ushered into Duska's parlour shortly before eight bells sounded.

Tilda stood up immediately to greet them. Thank Power Tego looked better than the last time she'd seen him, even if he was bandaged about the head and still worryingly pale. Zander's limp wasn't too bad either. Nico looked tired of course; she wasn't surprised, after all he'd had to do. Yanni and Timo appeared to be the most alert of the lot of them. A rush of affection flooded through Tilda and she smiled, trying to ignore her own fuzzy head and aching body.

"Thank you all for coming. I'm sorry we don't have long."

Time was ticking away; Duska had already been carried out to the cart in readiness for the ride back to the woods. She would have to keep this brief.

"I wanted to tell you all how much I appreciated you letting me work with you. I realise it wasn't easy, taking a powermage who was a complete novice into the mine, and making her a Worm. I'm afraid I wasn't very good at it."

"Ah, you made a passable Worm," Yanni said, winking at her.

"Between you, you taught me a lot." Tilda grimaced. "I could've done without the rockfall, though."

The team laughed then, until Nico interrupted. "I told them what you found."

"What?" He'd told the team about the silviron? That was supposed to be a secret.

"You know, the diamant," Nico added quickly, raising his eyebrows at her.

Relief flooded through Tilda. "Oh, that. Yes."

"It was real good of you, Tilda, to give it him," Zander said, and everyone nodded.

"It's cos of that, Nico's setting himself up as a Master," Yanni told her. "He's asked us all to work with him."

"Feliks won't be very pleased," Timo said.

"But he'll soon find himself another team," Tego finished for him.

"Really?" Tilda glanced over at Nico, who was trying not to look too smug. "So does that mean you're going to dress up and sit in an office?"

Nico snorted. "Not likely. I'll be a Master-miner. Working down the mine with my team."

Zander grinned. "I think I'm going to like working for a Master with a nose for stones."

"A nose, or an ear," Yanni muttered, but so quietly only Tilda heard him.

In the distance came the sound of bells striking. As if on cue, Isaak stuck his head round the door. "Time to go, Tilda. Best finish up."

"Oh, of course." Tilda shook hands with everyone. Nico was the last to leave; as she let go of his hand, she asked him something she'd been wondering. "Is Feliks alright? I thought he might have come to say goodbye too."

"He's fine." Nico chuckled. "A bit embarrassed perhaps."

Tilda wrinkled her nose in confusion. "Why embarrassed?"

"Well, it's not good for a Master's ego when you're found by your secretary, trussed up and locked in a broom cupboard in just your underthings. Samya knocked him out cold, apparently."

Tilda couldn't help giggling, but then she grew serious. "So when I went to the office with Yanni, to tell Feliks about the black ruby, he was locked in a cupboard? If only we'd got back to the office quicker, we might have prevented Samya . . . well, Luisa . . . doing that to him."

"But if you had, you wouldn't have ended up down the mine again and found silviron or the diamant," Nico said. "And I wouldn't be looking at becoming a Master with my own team."

"True."

Nico grinned. "You know, if ever you fancy giving up the maging business, you could come and work for me. With two of us listening out for stonesong, there's no telling how many velvets we could find."

"Ha! I don't think the other mages would be too pleased about me deserting them to dig up stones. Although it does sound like it might be easier at times," Tilda admitted.

Nico frowned. "Is Luisa a real threat? For Issraya, I mean?"

"Honestly?" Tilda sighed when Nico nodded. "I think so. She will be in possession of so much dark magic, especially now she's got Arkanal's ruby. Finding the silviron was only one of the things we needed to do, to try to stop Luisa taking over. We've still got to get safely back to Ring Isle, try to repair the Ringstone . . ." She paused and shook her head. "If we can't get the Ringstone working properly again, I don't know how we can access the Power to fight her."

"You'll do it, I'm sure. Look at what you've achieved by yourself. You saved the Mage of Pergatt, dug up a singing stone and starmetal, *and* made a pretty good Worm into the bargain. Power knows, you'll manage even more between the five of you."

"I hope so." The future was still too uncertain for Tilda to sound optimistic. Who knew what Luisa was capable of? She wouldn't think about that. Not yet, anyway. Quickly, she changed the subject. "Have you decided what colour your team neckers are going to be?"

"I have. And as an honorary member of the team"—Nico pulled from his pocket a large piece of blood-red fabric—"you get one too. This isn't a proper one, but I couldn't let you go without it. The colour will remind you of a certain ruby, even if we can't tell the rest of the world about it." He hung the material around Tilda's neck and tied it in a loose knot.

She toyed with its ends. "Thank you."

"I've got something else for you, too." Nico handed her a small white velvet bag. "It's not the very best of its kind, and it's certainly worth a fraction of the diamant's value, but I thought you might like it."

Tilda tipped the bag up; a small flattened oval with a hole in one end fell into her hand.

"It's a seastone," Nico told her. "I thought it was appropriate, seeing as how you're the Mage of Merjan."

The stone's flat surfaces were slightly ridged, striped in shades of blue, and speckled with white.

"I can see how it got its name." Tilda turned the stone so that it caught the light and the stripes looked even more like waves. "It's beautiful."

"I drilled the hole so you can wear it if you want to. There's a cord in the bag."

"Oh, yes! Would you . . . ?"

Nico knotted the cord to the stone, and Tilda slipped the necklace over her head. The stone sat comfortably below her throat; she rested her fingers on it, strangely relieved to find it had no stonesong. "Thank you, Nico."

"Tilda, are you coming?" Silviu called.

"Yes, I'm coming." Tilda was suddenly aware of being a powermage again. She wanted to give Nico a hug, but she ought to maintain a distance. Instead, she grabbed Nico's work-roughened hand and shook it for the last time before she hurried out of the parlour and out of Duska's house.

The cart and horse were waiting outside the door, and so were Sasha and the rest of the mining team. Tilda climbed up into the back of the cart and squeezed herself next to the mattress on which Duska lay covered in blankets.

Duska opened her eyes and reached out. "Silviu told me," she whispered as Tilda took the proffered hand. "Well done." She gave Tilda's fingers a squeeze.

Silviu climbed up next to Isaak and twisted round on his seat. "Are we all set?"

"All set," Tilda said.

The cart gave a jolt, and began to move.

"Goodbye, my Lady," Sasha called.

"Goodbye, Tilda. Bye," Nico shouted.

"Goodbye! Thank you." Tilda called and waved, and ignored the emptiness in her chest at leaving the team behind, until the cart turned the corner and she couldn't see them any more. She sank down into the cart and hugged her mining memories close as the wheels ate up the miles beneath her.

Chapter 26
Repair

IT HAD BEEN three days since Tilda stepped through the door deep in the heart of the Pergattian forest and into Gemsman Georj's strong room once more.

A carriage had been waiting outside the shop to take them straight to the docks, Taimane already sitting inside it with a folderful of paperwork from the Historykeepers. And the *Silver Fish* had been waiting for them at the docks, a tent erected on her deck to provide shelter and privacy for Duska on the journey back to Ring Isle.

To Tilda's surprise, Gemsman Georj came with them.

"He has the expertise and knowledge to help us," Silviu told her. "We have to remove the tainted silviron from the Ringstone before we can replace it." He tapped the lid of the wooden box which, Tilda knew, contained the lump of starmetal.

And now, after three days of being pampered by Aunt Tresa and doing nothing but eating and resting, Tilda was back in the Ring Room with the other powermages and Georj.

She stared down at the empty circles on the top of the Ringstone, playing subconsciously with the seastone she'd taken to wearing all the time. Georj had removed every last trace of the tainted starmetal, chipping and scraping with his fine tools until only the black stone was left. Every little bit of the silviron he'd recovered had been placed into a lead casket, which Silviu had locked away in his apartment until the powermages could decide—together—what to do with it.

It had been bad enough seeing one empty circle when the Ambakian ring had been sent back to its homeland, but to see all five gone . . . Tilda found herself trembling. "Will it work?"

"It should." Duska's voice sounded strong, but her pale face showed she was still far from well. She sat beside Kamen, on a couch that had been brought into the Ring Room specially; neither were at full strength and able to stand for long periods yet. "But unless the Power knows different, this is the last of the silviron. We cannot allow it to be tainted, ever again."

There was a lit brazier beside the Ringstone; Silviu held his hand out over it, testing. "Is it hot enough yet?"

Georj carefully fed the brazier; his sleeves were rolled up, and a sheen of sweat coated his brow. "Not quite. The crucible isn't ready. It needs to be cherry red before we can proceed."

Tilda looked at the ceramic cup sitting atop the coals. It glowed orange.

Satisfied with the amount of wood he'd added, Georj tied a leather apron around his waist and pulled on a pair of heavy leather gloves. "It won't be long, now."

"Are you certain there's no chance of contamination?" Taimane looked up from the document he'd been reading. "Nothing left of the old stuff and no other metals?"

Georj nodded. "I even removed a thin layer of stone to be absolutely sure. The melting cup has never been used before, and the tongs have been covered. Look." He held up a pair of curved tongs, their gripping claws wrapped round and round with strips of leather.

"It's red," Tilda said, pointing.

Sure enough, the ceramic pot was glowing almost the same colour as the coals.

"Right. This is it then." Silviu glanced round at everyone. "Are we all ready?"

Tilda nodded and moved closer to the brazier. Its heat was intense, burning her face. No wonder Georj was sweating.

"Lord Taimane, if you would be so good as to man the bellows?" Georj smiled. "Lord Silviu, if you wouldn't mind . . . the box?"

Silviu opened the wooden box and Tilda's breath caught in her chest. There it was—the new silviron, sitting on a cushion of white velvet, glinting softly and reflecting the fiery glow of the brazier.

"Thank you." Georj manouvered the tongs around the lump and lifted it out. Carefully, he placed it into the waiting crucible.

Nothing happened.

Tilda's chest tightened. "It's not working."

"It takes a little time to heat through. Have patience." Georj inspected the embers. "Lord Taimane, can I relieve you of the bellows for a moment?"

"Definitely." Taimane relinquished them with apparent relief.

Under Georj's expert hands, the embers turned white. If that wasn't hot enough to melt silviron . . .

Tilda edged as close to the brazier as she could bear to be, screwing her face up against the heat. Inside the crucible, the lump of silviron began to glow orange. Then it seemed to shiver. "Something's happening!"

As she watched, the orange deepened to red. The surface folds in the silviron smoothed out, the volume of the lump shrinking as the metal liquefied. It seemed to take an age before the silviron was completely melted, but the crucible ended up half full of shimmering, red, molten starmetal.

It didn't look much in this state. Was there even enough to refill the empty circles in the top of the Ringstone?

Georj set the bellows aside and picked up the tongs again. Lifting the crucible from the embers, he watched the contents carefully.

Tilda saw its colour deepen, the bright red darkening to the colour of blood and then to red-grey.

As soon as it reached that point, Georj quickly turned and poured the rapidly cooling liquid into the waiting circle of rings.

It was exactly the same as when Tilda had replaced the lost ring; the liquid metal ran easily along the channels carved into the Ringstone, filling them evenly. Any remaining redness faded until all that remained was the familiar silver-grey, speckled with sparkles. And at first sight, thank Power, no sign of any purple-black shadows.

An intense silence filled the room, then Silviu gave a bellow of a laugh and slapped Georj on the back. "You've done it!"

The gemsman inclined his head and wiped the sweat from his brow. "Thank Power."

"Are you sure the conduit is restored?" Duska pushed herself to her feet, and after accepting Taimane's proffered arm, walked the few shaky steps from her seat to the Ringstone. She gripped its edge for support. "There's no haze."

It was true. But the silver haze that hovered above the Ringstone wasn't always present. It didn't mean there was no Power getting through. Tilda chewed at her lip. Or did it?

"We won't know for sure until we try to draw." Kamen joined Duska at the stone and turned to Georj. "We are grateful for your assistance, Gemsman, but we must ask you to leave us now. For your own safety."

For his safety? What about theirs? An icy shiver ran down Tilda's back as she remembered what she'd been told the first time she watched the powermages draw Power; one wrong word in the chanting can do all sorts of damage to those closest to the Ringstone if the Power can't be contained.

Power only knew what would happen if there was still anything wrong with the Ringstone and they tried the incantation.

Georj bowed. "I understand. There is only so much I can do, and my part is already played. I hope it has achieved what you needed it to."

As the door to the Ring Room closed behind Georj, Silviu glanced at his fellow mages. "Are we ready to try?"

"No point in waiting." Taimane's moustache twitched. "If the conduit's not sufficiently repaired and we can't draw Power this way, we'll need a major rethink. Best find out sooner rather than later."

Kamen nodded. "Together, then."

On Silviu's signal, Tilda reached out with the others and laid her hand gently on the Merjanian ring. It was still slightly warm, but that's all she could feel. There was nothing to see either. No silvery haze or coloured lights.

No Power.

It hadn't worked. After everything that had happened, everything she'd been through, it hadn't worked. Did they need something extra to draw the Power out?

"Hastel athor, embarak nouray," Silviu muttered.

"Ilsteth horat umbaroth," Tilda joined in, repeating the words she'd spoken at her initiation. If all five powermages recited the incantation, perhaps words would succeed where touch alone was failing?

Aahhh . . .

It was as though someone had set off fireworks; the familiar auras burst out of the Ringstone, filling the space above it with bright colour. Almost immediately, strands of light representing the different portions wrapped themselves around their respective mages.

Tilda laughed out loud as her portion crashed into her body, pounding her with waves of Power, setting every nerve tingling and fizzing. She looked around at the other mages; she didn't know if everyone experienced Power in the same way that she did, but it was obvious that it was having an effect.

Duska had her eyes closed, almost as though she was basking in summer sunlight, and there was already much more colour in her cheeks. Kamen was standing straighter and taller than he had for a while, and his eyes had their twinkle back. Taimane was twirling one end of his moustache with his free hand, which sent little purple sparks shooting past his ear. Silviu was grinning, his fist raised in triumph.

Hello again, Tilda.

She turned her attention to the Power as its voice spoke in her head.

You have done well, little powermage. I am grateful to you.

"Are you all right? Can you flow properly? I mean, there's nothing left of Luisa's taint? You'd tell me if there was, wouldn't you?" she gabbled.

The conduit is pure once more. The Power laughed. *I have not felt this . . . free . . . since before we portions were constrained to the Ringstone.*

"Not even when Luisa pulled you out of it?"

There was a soft sound, like the "shhhh" of waves drawing back across sand. Was that a Power equivalent of a sigh? *Not even then.*

"Good," Tilda replied in her head. Then she pulled a face. Luisa wasn't really a subject she wanted to talk about at this moment, but perhaps she ought to let the Power know what had happened. "The thing is . . ."

Yeeesss?

"Well . . . it's a good job we can draw on you again because . . . we really need you. It's Luisa. Again."

Oh?

How could she say this? "There was a black ruby . . . The miners found it, by accident. But she took it." Tilda braced, waiting for the Power's reaction.

A moment of stillness and then—

Thin strands of purple and green, red and yellow light shot up from the ring underneath Tilda's hand, wrapping themselves around separate fingers.

She gasped. Not again!

A chorus of different voices filled her head for the second time in a week.

Arkanal's ruby?

We know of it.

But we have not been troubled by it for millennia.

Luisa has it?

Tilda nodded. "Yes."

Then the powermages must stay alert. The black ruby by itself cannot overthrow us, but the one who holds it can bring great harm.

"I know. I'm sorry, it's my fault. I didn't stop her."

Do not blame yourself, Tilda Benjasson. We are confident that you will have done all that you could. And if it were not for you, we would not be here, now, ready to serve the powermages and protect Issraya again.

Tilda stared down at the five auras twisted around her fingers. "How can you all be connected to me at the same time, through the Merjanian ring? I thought you had to be shared between the mages. You did it before, though, didn't you? In the cavern, when I touched the silviron."

We go where we need to be, Tilda Benjasson. You needed all of us to be able to remove the silviron, so we filled you. We need you now, because you bring a warning about Luisa.

"But you've not done this to the other mages." Tilda glanced around the Ringstone; not one of her fellow mages seemed to be aware that a little of their portions was connected to and speaking directly with a mage from a different region.

No. Your inexperience is . . . useful. No one has told you what isn't possible, so you don't expect to fail. Bear that in mind, Tilda Benjasson, when you are tested in future and need to use us.

The voices faded, the thinner strands unwrapped themselves from Tilda's fingers, and then there was only the blue light and voice of her own portion left.

Be sure to always fill completely, Tilda. And know that all of us will be here when you need us again, but you had best keep that knowledge to yourself for the moment.

Tilda's eyes widened. "I can't even tell Silviu?"

To yourself, Tilda. Keep it to yourself. Now draw . . .

It couldn't be right not to tell the other powermages, she thought, drawing her portion into herself and feeling the familiar fizz build inside her body. Why would the Power even ask her to keep such a secret?

Silviu waved a hand in front of Tilda's face, interrupting her thoughts. He indicated she should break the connection.

"The Power's flowing well," he said, looking pleased. "So I think we can be pretty certain that the conduit is repaired and working properly. Is everyone refilled?"

"Back in business," Taimane replied, rubbing his hands together.

"I feel twenty years younger," Kamen said, and Tilda couldn't help smiling, because he looked it.

Duska flexed her fingers. "Shadow threads? What shadow threads?"

"And you, Tilda?" Silviu waited for her reply.

"Me? Oh, fine. Full of fizz."

Silviu chuckled. "Good. None of this would have been possible without you, Tilda. You've done very well." He bowed to her, and the others followed suit.

Tilda's cheeks grew hot. Was it due to a flush of pleasure because of their appreciation, or a rush of guilt, because of the secret she was hiding from them?

"I think a celebration is in order." Taimane rubbed his stomach. "I have a hankering for the best that Marja can rustle up in the castle's kitchen." He walked towards the door.

"I agree." Kamen followed him.

"Gemsman Georj deserves an invitation to the party. And a toast or two," Duska said, linking arms with Silviu. There was a definite spring in her step as she pulled him across the room.

Tilda stayed where she was, staring at the silvery haze now floating above the Ringstone. Yes, they ought to celebrate. They were able to draw Power again through an untainted silviron conduit, and would continue to meet the needs of the people of Issraya.

But Luisa was still out there somewhere, she had the black ruby, and Tilda couldn't help thinking that at some point in the future, they'd be facing her again. How would she use the black ruby's power? Would she try to take the Power to herself again? Or would she try to destroy the mages first?

A hand fell on her shoulder, making her jump. She looked up, into Duska's smiling face.

"Tilda, is everything alright?"

"Yes. Yes, I was just looking . . ." Tilda waved a hand in the direction of the Ringstone.

"It's good to know it's working again, isn't it? We are so privileged. No one except the five powermages will ever experience it." Duska squeezed Tilda's shoulder and walked back to where Silviu waited for her.

Tilda hesitated. It wasn't fair of her to spoil this moment with dark thoughts. She wasn't going to have to face Luisa alone, was she? There were four other mages to keep that particular threat at bay, and Tilda had received the Power's assurance that all five portions would come to her aid if ever she needed them, just like they had before, in the mine. Although she hoped it would never come to that.

She stared down at the haze again, and at the restored circle of rings set into the Ringstone's flat top. Her hand strayed to the seastone necklace; one day she'd ask Silviu how to put Power into it. Then she'd always have something to fall back on if things got tough.

"Tilda, come on!"

Tilda took one last look at the Ringstone. Together—Power *and* powermages—they would face whatever happened next.

"Coming," she called, and ran to join her fellow mages.

Katherine Hetzel has always loved the written word, but only started writing "properly" after giving up her job as a pharmaceutical microbiologist to be a stay-at-home mum. The silly songs and daft poems she wrote for her children grew into longer stories. They ended up on paper and then published. (*Granny Rainbow*, Panda Eyes, 2014, *More Granny Rainbow*, Panda Eyes, 2015) Her debut novel, *StarMark*, was published by Dragonfeather in June 2016 and her second stand-alone novel, *Kingstone*, in June 2017. The first book of *The Chronicles of Issraya* was published in 2019. She sees herself first and foremost as a children's author, passionate about getting kids reading, but she also enjoys writing short stories for adults and has been published in several anthologies. A member of the online writing community Den of Writers, Katherine operates under the name of Squidge and blogs at Squidge's Scribbles. She lives in the heart of the UK with Mr Squidge and two children.